"I fantasized ab

just like this one," Beth said, pressing a quick kiss to his lips, then whirling away.

"Did you?" Chance asked, closing the distance between them, drawing her against him. Even in the dark he could see her blush.

"I don't get out much." She pressed her hands to his chest. "You can probably tell."

"I find that hard to believe." Chance wrapped a piece of her fiery, shiny hair around his finger and brought it to his nose. The ocean hadn't stolen her own sweet scent, but combined with it to create something at once feminine and wild. "You're so beautiful tonight," he said, lowering his eyes to her mouth.

Beth sobered, the laughter dying on her lips. She shook her head. "I've never been beautiful. Never been . . . alluring."

"No?" He slipped his hands from her shoulders to the small of her back, to softer curves and beyond. "You are alluring . . . and exciting." He moved his lips to her ear, to the pulse that beat wildly just behind it. "You are driving me mad with need."

Beth moaned and leaned into him. "Then kiss me, Chance. Show me the way I make you feel. . . ."

WHAT ARE *LOVESWEPT* ROMANCES?

They are stories of true romance and touching emotion. We believe those two very important ingredients are constants in our highly sensual and very believable stories in the *LOVESWEPT* line. Our goal is to give you, the reader, stories of consistently high quality that may sometimes make you laugh, sometimes make you cry, but are always fresh and creative and contain many delightful surprises within their pages.

Most romance fans read an enormous number of books. Those they truly love, they keep. Others may be traded with friends and soon forgotten. We hope that each *LOVESWEPT* romance will be a treasure—a "keeper." We will always try to publish

LOVE STORIES YOU'LL NEVER FORGET
BY AUTHORS YOU'LL ALWAYS REMEMBER

The Editors

Loveswept 599

Erica Spindler
Tempting Chance

BANTAM BOOKS
NEW YORK · TORONTO · LONDON · SYDNEY · AUCKLAND

TEMPTING CHANCE

A Bantam Book / February 1993

If you would be interested in receiving protective vinyl
covers for your Loveswept books, please write to this address
for information:

Loveswept
Bantam Books
P.O. Box 985
Hicksville, NY 11802

ISBN 0-553-44366-6

Published simultaneously in the United States and Canada

Bantam Books are published by Bantam Books, a division of
Bantam Doubleday Dell Publishing Group, Inc. Its trademark,
consisting of the words "Bantam Books" and the portrayal of
a rooster, is Registered in U.S. Patent and Trademark Office
and in other countries. Marca Registrada. Bantam Books, 666
Fifth Avenue, New York, New York 10103.

PRINTED IN THE UNITED STATES OF AMERICA

OPM   0 9 8 7 6 5 4 3 2 1

For Cynthia:
Sisters always,
Friends at last

Prologue

Elizabeth Lucille Waters was born September 4, at 3:57 A.M. The day also happened to be Labor Day, appropriately, and it wasn't until after twenty hours that little Beth made her grand entrance. Or exit, as it were. Her parents were delighted with both their daughter and her method of arrival; both believed that hard work was the cornerstone of existence and that nothing good came without sweat.

In that case, little Beth was very, very good.

Her maternal grandmother, Eva, flew in from the West Coast for the big event, although she arrived two and a half weeks late. After all, playing the lead in a small company's production of *Mame* could, with luck, parlay into something much grander; one didn't walk away from those opportunities, even for the birth of one's first grandchild.

The show must go on.

Upon arriving in Kansas, the former Eugenia McClowsky, also of the Land of Oz, was totally undone to learn that her daughter and "that *accountant*" she'd married had decided to call the child Beth.

The actress decided on the spot that she couldn't have it. Beth was too ordinary, too everyday a name for *her* grandchild, this infant with carrot-red curls and huge blue eyes.

Holding the cooing child above her, the actress proclaimed, "I shall call you Liza."

One

It was the "or else" that always got her.

Beth Waters stared down at the chain letter she held in her hands, rereading its contents. The letter promised all manner of reward—or retribution—depending on her response to its demands. According to this one, breaking the chain had even resulted in death.

Superstitious claptrap, no doubt about it. Mail extortion, definitely. But still . . . Beth caught her bottom lip between her teeth, acknowledging her uneasiness, acknowledging the feeling of being "or elsed" into something she didn't want to do.

Well, not this time. Beth inched her chin up a notch. She wouldn't be bullied. She wouldn't be threatened by someone else's superstitions or idea of a sick gag. Crumpling the letter, she tossed it into the trash.

There! Beth squared her shoulders. That felt good. Great, even. Eva—her flamboyant actress grandmother—was right. It was time she developed some spunk. It was time she started living dangerously.

Smiling to herself, Beth turned her attention to where it should have been all along, Art One's stack of Monday morning mail, the mail it was her job as receptionist to separate and pass along.

As she began doing just that, her gaze strayed to the envelope in which the chain letter had come. She picked it up. Judging by the Laguna Beach postmark, somebody local had sent it. And, as it had come to the art brokerage, most likely someone who knew her through her job. One of the artists? A client? Coworker?

Beth made a sound of self-disgust as she realized what she was doing. She didn't care who'd sent the stupid thing. It was out of her mind. It was. She sent the envelope sailing down to join the letter.

The next hour passed quickly: she finished with the mail, took a dozen calls, and made a fresh pot of coffee. And, about a million times, she caught herself gazing at the wastebasket located just under her desk. Each time she did, she scolded herself for being a ninny and with the toe of her Mary Jane shoe, nudged the waste receptacle a bit farther under the desk.

Finally Beth gave up. Okay, she rationalized. She *was* buckling under. But she wasn't the only one; after all, someone had sent the letter to her. Someone who, no doubt, hated them as much as she did.

Besides, why take chances?

She bent and reached for the crumpled letter, only to find that she'd inched the wastebasket farther back than she could reach. Feeling more than a bit silly, she slid out of her chair and crawled under the desk to retrieve it.

"Beth!"

Startled, Beth jerked her head up, whacking it on the underside of the desk. Tears sprang to her eyes and, rubbing her head, she cursed her luck. The bellow belonged to Chance Michaels, owner of Art One. That he was her boss and a demanding, volatile perfectionist workaholic didn't rattle her.

That he was drop-dead gorgeous did. Big-time.

She squeezed her eyes shut and the image of his sharply defined face filled her head—square chin cut with a deep cleft; nose, Roman in character but not quite straight; mouth, full, generous, yet chiseled. His was a strong face, masculine, full of deviltry, full of fun.

As if a part of Chance Michaels refused to grow up.

That was the part of him she found impossible to resist, the part that kept her slightly off balance. Brash, bold, and boyish at the same time, Chance embraced life as if it were an exciting challenge; he knew how to have fun.

And women were drawn to him like hummingbirds to nectar. Beautiful women. Self-confident, powerful women. Women who knew what they wanted out of life and took it.

He even attracted receptionists who understood a man like Chance Michaels wouldn't look at them twice.

Beth took a deep breath. She would steel herself against his effect on her. Chance Michaels was just a man. As was her father. Her brother. The guy who delivered her bottled water. Nothing special about this one. Sure.

Head still smarting, Beth peeked over the top of the desk at him. Her heart crashed to her toes.

So much for plan A.

His velvety brown eyes crinkled at the corners as he grinned at her. "You okay? I was just about to call in the cavalry."

The curving of his lips was cocky to the point of

impudence. She felt the movement all the way to the tips of her toes. Heat flew to her cheeks and she cursed her redhead's translucent complexion. "I'm fine."

His grin widened. "You're sure?"

Beth rubbed her head again. "Uh-huh."

"Good."

He leaned against the door frame and folded his arms across his chest. She met his gaze evenly, determined not to let him fluster her. After a moment she lifted her eyebrows coolly and in question, congratulating herself on her own performance. "You needed me for something?"

"Mmm-hmmm." He cocked his head in amusement. "But first, is there something under there that I should know about? Something really great? A cockroach review? Dust balls on parade . . . ?"

He let his teasing question trail off, and the heat in her cheeks became fire. She was still on her knees and half under the desk! Good going, Waters, she thought. Cool as a cucumber, real smooth.

"Of course not." She straightened up and slipped back into her chair, making a great show of smoothing her skirt. "I was simply trying to get"—she held up the crumpled paper—"this."

Chance shook his head and crossed to her. "Move your trash can to the side of your desk so you don't have to dig for it."

He squatted down, retrieved the basket, then tipped his head back to look up at her. His eyes crinkled at the corners once again. "Nice legs, Red."

She stared at him. "Pardon?"

"Legs," he repeated. "Real showstoppers."

"Oh," she murmured, wishing some cocky and confident comeback would spring to her tongue.

Laughing softly, Chance stood back up. "I didn't

mean to embarrass you, Beth. I have this problem with saying what's on my mind."

"You didn't. Embarrass me, that is." She took a deep, steadying breath. "I know what a tease you are."

"Do you?" He gazed at her a moment more, then cleared his throat. "Any sign of my assistant?"

"Laura?" Beth asked, surprised. "Don't you remember? She quit. Friday." At his blank look, she rolled her eyes. "Big argument, she called you an arrogant, demanding—"

"I remember that part." He shook his head. "Didn't I ask you to call her and beg her to come back? Didn't we send flowers?"

"Yes and yes."

"And?"

Beth folded her hands in her lap. "You want the unvarnished truth?"

He looked at her, the solemnness of his expression belied by the mischief in his eyes. "I can take it."

"She said you could take your job—and your apology—and put them where the sun—"

"I get the picture." Chance glanced around them, taking in the crates of still-to-be-unpacked works, the stacks of ones needing to be recrated and shipped back to the artists. "Damn inconvenient timing." He met her gaze again. "How many does that make?"

"Assistants? Three in three months."

His expression changed, becoming intense, almost brooding. "Any suggestions? Besides an ad in the *L.A. Times* and patience pills, that is."

Beth gazed at him seriously. Thoughtfully. It was that intensity, the mood shifts, that made working for Chance difficult. But interesting as well. The job of Chance's assistant would be demanding. And challenging. Too bad Laura hadn't felt the same way.

Beth lifted her hands, palms up. "Sorry. But I'll place the ad right away."

"Thanks." He started for his office, then stopped and turned back to her. "Am I that bad to work for?"

"No," she said softly, horrified at the way her throat closed over the words. "No, you're not."

He smiled. "And Red?"

"Yes?"

"I wasn't just teasing. You do have great legs."

And then he was gone. Beth stared at his closed door for a full ten seconds before she realized she'd stopped breathing.

Legs. Chance smiled as he snapped his office door shut behind him. She had them, all right. Slim, strong, and shapely. Unbelievably, he hadn't noticed them before. He shook his head. Damn shame too. Legs like that tended to put a man in a good mood. And lately he'd been a bear.

No wonder Laura had quit. And the two assistants before her.

Chance crossed to his desk, a minimal affair made totally of glass. The entire office was done in light neutrals so as not to interfere with the artwork placed throughout—some pieces brilliantly, even shockingly colored, others subtly, evocatively understated.

Chance sat behind the desk and looked around him. All the art in this room belonged to his personal collection, each piece by an artist he not only represented but had discovered as well.

He moved his gaze from one painting to another, smiling as satisfaction warmed him. He loved finding and launching new talent. He'd made a bundle off each; these successes had earned him a reputation in the industry worth more than any amount of money.

But the satisfaction he felt had to do with more than either of those, he acknowledged. His love of launching new talent was more personal. More immediate. Chance shook his head. Maybe it had to do with the fact that his own parents had struggled so long to make a go of their art, maybe he loved it because it made him . . . What?

Feel. The word popped into his head, and he scowled.

Ridiculous.

Annoyed with himself and the train of his thoughts, he stood back up and began to move restlessly around the room. He turned his attention to the approaching Summer Show and his need for a brilliant yet undiscovered new talent. Every year the Summer Show at his San Francisco gallery served as a vehicle to launch an unknown into art stardom. Only this year, he hadn't found the right talent, this year everything had looked . . . mediocre.

Frowning, Chance stopped and stared at a bold slash of red in one of his favorite paintings, acknowledging the restlessness that never seemed to leave him. The feeling that something important was missing.

Ridiculous, he thought again. Nothing was missing. He had a great life, damn near perfect. He had the freedom to do what he pleased, freedom from emotional entanglements. He had the financial success that enabled him to act on whatever whim struck him, be it a woman, traveling, or high-tech toys.

Damn *near* perfect, he thought again, than made a sound of disgust.

Maybe he needed to get out. He swung back

toward his desk and the picture window beyond, squinting against the brilliant light. Call one of his women friends and go to San Francisco for the weekend. He could pay a visit to the gallery there, take in a few openings.

He hadn't been out with a woman since he'd broken off with Gizelle. Or had it been Monique who'd demanded that they deepen their relationship . . . or else?

He'd opted for the "or else." He always did.

How long ago had that been? Chance wondered, crossing to the window and the southern California sunshine that spilled abundantly through. Eight weeks? Twelve?

What the hell was wrong with him?

A movement outside caught his eye. Laughing, a child ran from her mother, a big red balloon bobbling behind her.

Red.

Beth.

Chance shook his head, thinking of how easily his receptionist flustered. And how prettily. He smiled. Red hair, blue eyes, and skin like fresh cream. With freckles. Lots of them.

He wondered if those freckles dotted more than her face, just as he'd wondered more than once if she blushed everywhere as deliciously as she did in her cheeks.

He'd never know, of course. She intrigued him because she was different from the women he usually surrounded himself with. And because he needed a change.

There, he'd admitted it. He was in a rut.

Chance rubbed the side of his nose with his index finger, his mouth lifting in self-directed amusement. After Monique or Gizelle, he couldn't remember which, he had considered asking Beth out. The notion had popped into his head one Friday afternoon when she'd peeked through his office door to say good night. The urge had come upon him so suddenly and so strongly that he'd been stunned.

He'd fought the urge off and been glad of it ever since. Getting involved with one's employees was a mistake, and Beth Waters wasn't the kind of woman a man asked out because he needed a change of pace. Women like Beth Waters looked for something different, something more permanent, than what a man like himself could offer.

Outside his window the mother caught up with the child. As she scooped the youngster into her arms, the balloon slipped from the child's fingers, was lifted by the breeze and taken.

"Chance?"

Startled, Chance turned. Beth had poked her head inside his office door. He met her gaze, and strangely unnerved by it, wondered if, somehow, she had read his thoughts. "Yes?"

"I knocked, but you didn't answer."

"I don't doubt it." He smiled. "You placed the ad?"

"Yes." She took a deep breath. "And while I was at it, I called the university's art department and arranged for a couple of graduate students to come over and help crate and uncrate the art out front. They'll be here after lunch."

"You're a miracle worker."

"Not so fast. I offered them twelve dollars an hour."

"I thought miracles were free."

"Not in southern California." She laughed and began backing out of his office. "I'll oversee their work and make sure the paintings get safely over to Benton and Brothers Advertising."

"What would I do without you?" She blushed wildly, and he grinned. "I mean that, Red."

Warmed with pleasure, she murmured, "Thanks."

Chance felt that one word like a punch to his gut; he felt the curving of her lips a bit lower. He told himself to get a grip.

"I'll let you know when the students get here."

"Do that."

"Do you need anything before I—"

"No."

"Okay. I'll—"

"Beth?"

She stopped. "Yes?"

The urge to invite her to dinner trembled on the tip of his tongue. Reminding himself of the kind of woman Beth Waters was, he swallowed the urge and instead murmured, "Thanks again."

And then she was gone.

Chance turned back to the window. The red balloon had long since disappeared into the field of blue sky, but for some reason, Chance found himself looking for it anyway.

"In your studio, just where I thought you'd be."

Pastel poised in mid-stroke, Beth looked up from the drawing in front of her. Her grandmother stood in the doorway, her expression amused.

Beth shifted her gaze from her grandmother to her watch and was shocked to see it was nearly nine. The last time she'd looked it had been six-fifteen and she'd been trying to put the embarrassing moment with Chance out of her mind.

Without a lot of success. Even now, thinking about it brought an image of how she must have looked on her hands and knees rummaging through a trash can.

Beth shook the image off, bringing her thoughts back to her grandmother. She drew her eyebrows together in confusion. Just yesterday, Eva had flown to New York to audition for a part on a soap opera. "When did you get back?"

The older woman flounced dramatically into the room. "This afternoon."

Beth slipped the pastel back into the box, then turned to face her grandmother. "How did it go?"

"Very well. Great, in fact." Eva bowed deeply, as if to an adoring audience. "It's between me and another actress, and although my agent warned me it may take awhile for the producers to make a decision, I was *much* better."

"Oh, Eva!" Beth jumped up and hugged her grandmother. "I'm so happy for you! You deserve this, you've worked so hard!"

Eva hugged her back, laughing. "I couldn't have done it without you." In an uncharacteristically grandmotherly gesture, Eva rubbed a smudge of pastel from Beth's cheek. "If you hadn't lent me the money for the trip—"

Beth waved away her thanks. "It was nothing."

"Nothing was your entire savings." Eva's already husky voice deepened. "Your rainy day fund."

Beth laughed. "I still have eighteen dollars and fifty-three cents. Besides, haven't you always told me that rainy day funds are for worrywart pencil pushers?"

"Like your father." Eva shuddered in dramatic disapproval, all traces of sentimentality gone.

Beth shook her head. "Dad's an accountant. And I'm changing the subject now."

"You always do that."

"Wouldn't you?"

Eva sniffed and crossed to Beth's work table and looked down at the work in progress. "New sketch?"

"You saw?" Beth asked, almost shyly.

"It's nothing short of fabulous."

Beth smiled, accustomed to Eva's exaggerations, especially when it came to her artwork. "I do think it's special. This whole series has me, I don't know . . . almost tingling with excitement. I know that sounds silly, but it feels like magic. Like something I conjured from outside myself."

"You know," her grandmother murmured, patting her sleek gray bob, "I've been thinking, why don't you ask your boss to take a look at your work? He's launched a lot of artists. I've heard that his instincts haven't failed him yet and that if he thinks you've got it, you have."

"No," Beth said quickly, a thread of panic curling through her at the thought of sharing her work. "It's too soon. I'm not ready."

Her grandmother made a sound of impatience. "You're never going to be discovered if you keep your work hidden in here."

"I don't want to be discovered," Beth said. "I just want—"

"To spend your life painting pictures no one will ever see," Eva supplied.

Color flooded Beth's cheeks, and she inched her chin up. "I make art because I have to. It's in here," she said softly, pressing her hand to her chest. "It's who I am. I don't do it because I'm a great talent or because I have a great vision to share with the world."

"But what if you do?" her grandmother countered. "What if—"

"You're my grandmother. You have to believe in me."

She and her grandmother always disagreed on this one point. It was ironic. Her parents had never believed in her or understood her need to create; her grandmother believed in her, but couldn't understand her fear of sharing that part of herself with others.

For a long time after her grandmother left, Beth brooded over what the older woman had said to her. Was her grandmother right? Would she spend her life painting pictures no one would see? Was that what she wanted?

It wasn't. But the alternative—showing and sharing her work—terrified her. Memories of all the times she'd put herself on the line and all the times she'd been rejected, came barreling back. Show her work to Chance? Ask him to evaluate it?

Beth shook her head, her chest tight. No. No way. She was who she was. Sure, she sometimes fantasized about being courageous, more like her freewheeling grandmother. Sometimes she let herself imagine being discovered.

But those were fantasies. She was shy, timid Beth. Quiet, reserved, cautious.

Only a fool would pretend to be someone she wasn't.

Two

The next morning Chance yawned as he watched the coffee drip from filter to pot. He'd worked late the night before, and here it was barely eight A.M. and he'd already been at Art One an hour.

So much for getting out of town for a weekend, he thought, rubbing the side of his just-shaved jaw. He couldn't even get home for a decent night's sleep. Finding a new assistant had better become a priority. Or he'd better move a cot in.

Chance yawned again, poured himself a cup of strong coffee, and started back to his office. He had to call the insurance company about the piece that had been damaged in transit yesterday. Considering the seriousness of the accident, they were damn lucky that more than the piece's glass and polished oak framing hadn't been ruined. After that, he needed to contact the artist who—

Chance's thoughts came to a sudden stop as he realized he was no longer alone. Beth sat at her desk in the reception area, craning to see in a small mirror as she French-braided her hair. Her fingers moved quickly, slipping over and through the fiery strands. Her hair, wavy to the point of crinkly, looked soft and fine, like the hair of a wayward angel.

He wondered how those strands would feel against his own fingers.

Fatigue forgotten, Chance trailed his gaze over the rest of her. Beth Waters was . . . cute. He shook his head, smiling. Most women would hate that description—hell, maybe Beth would as well. But, with her gamine, heart-shaped face, perky nose, and riot of freckles, it fit.

But for her mouth. Soft and full and the color of a sweet blush wine, her lips brought to mind many descriptions, cute not among them. Promising. Sensual. Totally distracting.

His gaze lingered, his gut tightened. Would those lips taste as luscious as they looked?

Realizing the direction of his thoughts, Chance frowned and jerked his gaze away from her mouth. Her clothes were simple, a short-sleeved white blouse with a small, frilly collar, a navy cardigan thrown over the back of her chair, and, he'd guess, a damnably long navy skirt. Her cosmetics and jewelry were as understated—plain, really—as her garments.

Plain. Prim. Shy. The adjectives fit the picture; nothing in her behavior suggested a woman other than the one she presented. But, for him, something didn't add up. Maybe it was her hair, darker than carrot but not quite auburn, or the speed with which her cheeks could heat. Fire. It was there; he was certain of it.

Still waters ran deep.

Chance laughed to himself at both the cliché and the pun. And at his own imagination. Beth Waters was exactly what she seemed to be. He really did need to get a new assistant.

He took a step toward her. "Good morning."

Beth jerked her head up, startled.

Chance looked over his shoulder, then down at himself. "Did I sprout horns or something?"

She blinked. "No, I just didn't expect to see you so early."

Chance laughed. "Until I find a new assistant, I'm afraid it's going to be in early and out late for me." He crossed to her desk, then rested on a corner. "I'm going to be a very dull boy."

Beth swallowed—hard. Maiden aunts were dull. Ironing was dull. Chance Michaels couldn't be dull if his life depended upon it. Even though the blood thrummed crazily through her veins, she said evenly, "Is there something I can do for you?"

"No." He leaned toward her, wondering if her skin would feel as soft as it looked. "What must you think of me, Ms. Waters?" he teased, arching his eyebrows. "Care to share?"

"I think I'll pass." She folded her hands on top of the chain letter, hoping he wouldn't notice it. "Can I get you some coffee?"

Chance held up his cup, then took a sip, studying her over the rim. She looked like a child with her hand caught smack-dab in the middle of a no-no. "What brings you in so early?"

"Nothing special." She cursed the guilty answer the minute it passed her lips. "Just trying to catch up on . . . things."

She lowered her gaze to the desk in front of her, then, as if realizing what she'd done, lifted it quickly back to his. Chance bit back a sound of appreciation. Did she have any idea how guileless her eyes were? Or how appealing that lack of artifice was?

He motioned to the paper in front of her. "What's that?"

"What's what?"

"This." He pinched the paper's corner and slid it out from under her folded hands, then scanned its contents. "A chain letter?"

Beth snatched it back. "That's right."

"Covering your bases, huh?"

She glared up at him. "I don't believe I asked your opinion."

"Hey"—Chance held his hands up—"I wouldn't want to get hit by a bus either. This is pretty frightening stuff."

Beth let out her breath in a huff. "Don't you have work to do?"

"Lots of it. But I'm having a lot more fun sitting here talking to you."

She tried glaring at him again, but he only poked through the stack of papers on her desk. "Mail hasn't come yet?"

He knew darn well it hadn't. "I'm not going to dignify that with an answer."

"No mail." He grinned. "Okay then, any calls?" At her expression he laughed. "All right, all right, I'll leave you alone." Chance started to stand, then stopped as he saw an edge of brilliant color peeking out from the stack of white papers on Beth's desk. "What's this?"

Her sketches. Beth stared at them, horrified. Along with the chain letter, they'd been stuffed into the portfolio she'd brought this morning. She'd thought nothing of taking them out, had meant to slip them back in as soon as she'd finished with the letter.

Now Chance had them.

Mouth dry, pulse hammering in her head, Beth watched as Chance picked up the drawings and studied them. It took all her control to keep from snatching them from his hands.

One second became two, then became minutes. To Beth it seemed like years, centuries even. The silence between them deafening, she wished he would say something, anything.

"Whose are they?" he asked finally.

Beth wetted her lips. No words of praise, no opinion. Her chest ached; each breath hurt. "Those?"

"Yes." Chance smiled and lifted the drawings. "These." He paused, his smile slipping. "Beth? Is something wrong?"

"No. They're my sister's sketches," she said quickly, the words popping out before she could stop them. "My sister . . . Liza."

"Liza," Chance repeated, as if testing the name on his tongue.

"Yes. I brought them by mistake." Beth held out her hand for the drawings. "She'd be furious if she knew I had them."

Ignoring her outstretched hand, Chance continued to study the drawings. He drew his eyebrows together. "I didn't know you had a sister, one who's an artist, no less."

"It never came up." Dear heavens, what had she gotten herself into? And how was she going to get out?

"Until now," he murmured, lowering his gaze once more to the drawings.

What did he think of them? Beth wondered, wishing he would either put down the drawings or say something. Anything. But he continued to study the sketches in silence.

She folded her arms across her chest. "We're nothing alike," she offered nervously, needing to fill the silence. "She . . . Liza, that is, is daring and outgoing. A real character."

"Like your grandmother."

Beth drew her eyebrows together, forgetting for a moment that he had met Eva, that her grandmother occasionally dated one of his best-selling artists. "Yes," she said finally. "But I'm more like my—I mean *our*—mother."

She struggled to keep from grabbing the sketches and stuffing them back into the portfolio. Blasted thing! Why hadn't she taken the time to check what was in it before she'd brought it this morning?

"These are roughs?"

"Yes. For paintings."

"Mmm." He cocked his head and her breath caught. "What's her medium, do you know?"

"Mixed. Acrylics mostly, some xerography and graphite. Whatever it takes. She's just started using oils as well."

He nodded without commenting. "Scale?"

"Large. Four foot by six. Some larger, some smaller."

Chance dropped the sketches to the desk. "They have a nice depth."

Depth. Beth's heart lurched. He thought they had depth. If Chance Michaels thought they had depth, she wasn't a failure; her parents had been wrong.

She released her pent-up breath in an excited rush. "She's trying to show, through color, shape, and transparency, something of the human condition." Hands shaking, Beth pointed to an area of the sketch. "By juxtaposing this heavy, dark element with this light, colorful one, she's pictorializing the great balancing act of life. You know—love and fear, alienation and connection. We're all human and we all belong to one family, yet so often we exist in a state of separation."

Beth lifted her gaze back to his only to find him staring quizzically at her.

"You two must be very close," he murmured.

"Why do you say that?"

"You know her work so well. Not many siblings get quite so involved in the other's creative expression."

She stared at him a moment, horrified at how tangled this situation had already become. "I am . . . very close to Liza." That, at least, wasn't a total fabrication—she couldn't get any closer.

"And you love her work."

"Yes, I do."

Chance cocked his head, and his dark hair tumbled over his forehead. "I always wondered what it would have been like to have a brother or sister."

He seemed to be waiting for some sort of reply, so she smiled brightly. "It's nice."

Chance stood. "Maybe I'll meet your Liza sometime. I'd enjoy talking to her about her paintings."

"No!" At his expression, Beth cleared her throat. "I mean, that's not likely. She's away a lot. Right now she's . . . biking through the mountains."

"Really? Which ones?"

Beth stared blankly at him. "Which ones, what?"

He smiled and shook his head. "Mountains, Beth."

"Oh." Beth paused, searching her memory for mountain ranges, wondering which ones people biked through. She took a stab. "The Rockies."

He lifted his eyebrows. "She is daring."

After he walked away, Beth lowered her gaze to the chain letter and glared at it. Terrific. Now her boss thought she had a sister. A sister he wanted to meet. If she'd just left the offensive letter in the garbage yesterday, she wouldn't be in this predicament. No doubt Eva would find this whole situation amusing.

Muttering an oath, Beth ripped the letter in half and dropped it into the trash. This time it would stay there.

Besides, she didn't see how her luck could get any worse than it already was.

Three days later Beth realized she'd been wrong. Her luck could get worse. Much worse. Near tears, she rested her forehead on her steering wheel, trying to ignore the cacophony of horns from the cars stuck behind her.

Until this morning the wave of bad luck could almost have been called a ripple of petty annoyances. Then Mr. Willy, her goldfish, had gone belly-up, and her utilities had been cut off because crazy old Mrs. Beaver from next store had been collecting her mail again. Now her heap of a car was dead, and she was stuck on the Santa Ana Freeway in bumper-to-bumper traffic.

Eventually Beth made it to a service station. There she learned from the mechanic that it would take more to fix her old beater than it was worth. Left with a decision—try to live in southern California without a car or take out a loan to buy another car in worse condition than the one that had just croaked—Beth chose financial poverty and wheels.

Exhausted from the daylong ordeal, Beth turned into the lot adjacent to her flamingo-pink stucco apartment building. Mrs. Beaver, still in her paisley print housecoat and slippers, was out front watering the geraniums. The woman stopped and gaped at her as if she were a complete stranger.

"New car," Beth called, stepping out of it. "My other one died on the freeway this morning."

Still her neighbor stared. Beth cleared her throat as she crossed to her. "Is something wrong, Mrs. Beaver?"

"I thought you moved."

"Moved?" Beth shook her head and hiked her purse strap onto her shoulder. "No. Just went to work."

"Then who moved?"

Not up to one of Gretchen Beaver's fantasies, Beth started inching toward the front steps. "Don't know. Sorry."

She reached the stairs then and grabbed the railing like a lifeline. "See you later, Mrs. Beaver."

With a final wave, Beth darted into the building. Keys in hand, she jogged up the stairs. She stopped short at the top, her heart rapping uncomfortably against her ribs. Her apartment door stood ajar, and light tumbled from the opening into the dim hallway. She'd locked her door this morning, she knew she had. Tightening her fingers on her keys, Beth took a cautious step toward the door. Then another. When she reached it, she slowly pushed it open.

Her heart stopped beating altogether, then started again with a vengeance. She'd been robbed. Folding her arms across her chest, Beth propelled herself into the now-empty apartment, stopping in the very center of her empty living room.

"I told you you'd moved."

Startled, Beth gasped and swung around. Her neighbor stood in the doorway, a dripping watering can in her right hand. Beth drew in a steadying breath. "Mrs. Beaver, were you here when this happened? Did you see the thieves?"

Mrs. Beaver frowned. "Didn't see no thieves. Moving men. They were here this morning."

"This morning," Beth repeated, light-headed. "What time?"

"Don't know. Early." Her neighbor looked around. "They gave me a card."

The older woman fished in her pocket for it, then handed it to Beth. The card read:

TRUSTY'S MOVING SERVICE
WE MOVE IT FAST!

They sure did.

"Mrs. Beaver . . . Gretchen, you have to go." Beth took the woman's arm and led her to the door. "Now is not a good time. In fact, it's a really bad time. We can talk . . . later. Much, much later."

After once again assuring the woman that she had no intention of moving, Beth shut the door and, with trembling fingers, twisted the dead bolt and fastened the safety chain.

Turning, she leaned against the door and for several moments stared at her empty apartment. A chill crawled up her arms, and she hugged herself. What was she going to do? She didn't have to check her insurance policy to know she was in deep trouble. The last time her policy had come due, she had canceled coverage on everything but . . . her studio.

Panic coursed through her and she raced through her living room to the back of the apartment. Dear Lord, what would she do if they had taken her paintings? She swung open the studio door, then stopped a dozen different emotions barreling over her, not the least of which was relief.

The thieves hadn't touched her studio. They'd taken her thirdhand couch and ten-year-old black-and-white TV, but they hadn't wanted her art. Even common criminals were art critics, Beth thought, hysterical laughter bubbling to her lips.

Giving in to the laughter, she laughed until she cried.

Only after Beth had cried herself dry did she realize what had happened—the letter, she'd broken the chain. She had to get it back.

Calling herself a superstitious idiot, she grabbed her purse and keys and headed for Art One.

Chance pulled into Art One's small, secluded parking area, pulling to a stop next to a beat-up car. He looked at it and frowned. At present he had two employees at this location: Virginia, his office manager and bookkeeper, who drove a Volvo sedan, and Beth, who drove some late-model compact. This car he'd never seen before.

Dammit. Chance flexed his fingers on the steering wheel. Not again. He'd been hit twice before, and the first time, the thieves—junkies—had been looking for drugs. They'd gotten Art One confused with the pricey veterinarian next door. Both times the criminals had irreparably damaged art in their frantic search for something whose value they could understand. The senseless destruction had made him sick.

Chance narrowed his eyes, searching the office's windows. They were dark save for a soft glow of light emanating from somewhere inside.

Not this time, he thought, suddenly furious. This time he'd caught the creeps red-handed. Picking up his cellular phone, he punched out 911 and reported the intruders. Then, instead of staying put as they'd ordered him to do, he slipped out of his car.

He wasn't about to sit still while criminals ransacked his business and destroyed irreplaceable works of art. No way.

Quietly, he shut the car door behind him and crept toward Art One's back entrance, muttering an oath as he saw the alarm's glowing green light. The thieves had neatly overridden the system. Again. What was the use of having the damn thing if it didn't keep criminals out?

He inched his way inside, going for the first available weapon he could find. He curled his fingers around a small, cylindrical sculpture called *Post-Modern Bird in Flight*, the polished bronze cold and smooth against his fingers.

Chance weighed the piece in his hand. From art object to blunt instrument—he hoped the artist had a sense of humor. He smiled grimly. And from art dealer to head-cracker. Nice.

Chance heard the intruder before he saw him. The creep was in the reception area, rifling through Beth's desk. Without making himself visible and in a voice he hoped sounded more ferocious than he felt, Chance called out, "Get down on your knees and put your hands behind your head. And before you think of trying anything funny, let me warn you, I'm armed and ready to use my weapon."

Chance heard a gasp. "I've called the police. They'll be arriving any moment."

The jerk whimpered, then said something that sounded like "Don't shoot."

Chance frowned. The intruder was a . . . woman? He eased slowly around the corner, peering into the darkened room. He took a step closer to the intruder, his sculpture up and at the ready. The whimper came again, followed by a whisper he couldn't quite make out.

But the voice sounded familiar. In fact, it sounded like—

"Beth?" he asked, lowering his arm. "Beth, is that you?

Chance took the croak as an affirmative, and crossed to her. She just looked up at him, on her knees, her hands cupped behind her head. He swore, helped her to her feet, then swore again. Pale and trembling, she was obviously scared witless.

Feeling like both monster and idiot, he drew her against his chest. "I'm so sorry, Beth," he murmured, stroking her hair, finding that it was as soft as he'd imagined it would be. "I saw the car and didn't recognize it. We've been hit before, and all I could think was . . ." Still she didn't make a sound and his voice trailed off. "I feel like a total jackass, Beth. Please, say something. At least let me know you're all ri—"

"Let the woman go, scumbag. And get your hands up!"

Three

It took five minutes to convince the police Chance wasn't a criminal. Then another five to assure them there wasn't a crime in progress. Through it all, Chance kept his arms around her.

Step out of his arms, she told herself. But even as her brain delivered the command, Beth pressed her head in the crook between his neck and shoulder, her hand to his chest. She breathed deeply. He smelled of soap and sweat and the leather of his jacket; his heart beat strong and sure under her palm. The combination intoxicated her and she pressed a fraction closer, breathing in again, allowing herself the pleasure, for she knew that in all probability she would never be this close to him again.

"Beth . . . honey, are you all right?"

Honey. No doubt he would use the term of endearment for any female who had collapsed into his arms, but still it made her feel special, made her feel as if she were special to him.

Calling herself an idiot, Beth smiled weakly. "I'm all right now. Thanks."

"You're sure?" He tightened his arms. "You're still trembling."

Relaxing her grip, she stepped away regretfully. "It's been a long day."

"And an exciting night." Chance laughed softly, and tucked some errant strands of her hair behind her ear. "What should we do for an encore?"

His fingers lingered; her pulse scrambled. Beth lowered her eyes. "I can't . . . imagine," she said, attempting to sound casual and getting breathless instead.

"Can't you?" Chance asked almost to himself, trailing his thumb along her cheekbone.

Beth shuddered at the touch, calling herself the liar she was. She could imagine, quite vividly and down to the smallest detail. Despite the fact that he would never be interested in a woman like her, her imagination could envision exactly how it would be between them.

Chance dropped his hand and took a step away from her. "I think we better get out of here." He gestured toward his office. "I need to get my brief-case, then I'll walk you out."

Beth realized that she hadn't moved, that she was still staring at him, and quickly swung toward her desk, pretending great interest in straightening it. How could she have behaved that way? she wondered, tears stinging the back of her eyes. He'd been concerned for her well-being, and she'd practically thrown herself at him. It would almost be funny if it didn't hurt so bad—mousy little receptionist swoons over gorgeous playboy boss.

She couldn't get more hokey or clichéd if she had written a script.

And all because of that stupid chain letter.

Beth sighed as she gazed at her now-chaotic desk.

The letter was long gone. The rational part of her had known that before she'd raced down here. Unfortunately, she hadn't been in the mood to listen to reason.

Hearing her sigh, Chance stopped at his office door and turned back to her. The desk lamp created a backdrop of light for her profile, turning her hair into a halo of fire, softening her already delicate features.

He cocked his head. She looked small and lost and . . . sad. Something twisted inside him, something in the vicinity of his heart, and suddenly he wanted to take her back into his arms. He wanted to hold her and stroke her until she forgot everything but him.

He wanted to make love to her.

Chance sucked in a sharp breath. How in the hell had his thoughts strayed so far from reality? Beth Waters was a woman who needed emotional commitment from a man. And that was something he could never give her. Or any woman.

Fatigue was playing havoc with his good sense.

Nothing more.

Sure. He and Beth had just shared an extraordinary, even harrowing, experience. It had brought out the Tarzan and Jane in both of them. An hour from now everything would be back to normal and he would wonder why he'd gotten himself all worked up.

"Beth?"

She looked up, her eyes large and vulnerable in her small face. That same place inside him ached, and he silently swore. Tarzan and Jane, he reminded himself. "Did you get what you came for?" he asked with forced casualness.

She shook her head. "No, but I'll make do."

"Maybe I can help you search? Let's see, what could you be looking for? Hmm . . ." He put his fingers to his head, swami-style, then closed his eyes. "This *is* southern California, so . . . my psychic powers tell me you're looking for your crystal pouch. No, no . . . it's your macrobiotic cookbook you search for. Wait—"

He glanced back up at her, relieved to see all traces of vulnerability gone from her expression—he found her vulnerability damn difficult to resist. "You're looking for your pet gecko, who also happens to be your good-luck talisman."

Beth burst out laughing, knowing with every fiber of her being that this night couldn't get any worse. "You should do this for a living."

"Which?" Chance crossed back to her, enjoying the tinkling sound of her laughter. It reminded him of the wind chimes on the porch of his beach house. "Stand-up comedy or psychic readings?"

"Both." She shook her head, still smiling. "And watch where you walk, I don't want you to squish Alfred."

"Alfred. Good name. Very dignified." He stopped beside her. "Are you ready?"

Beth nodded and they began moving toward the door. She glanced at him from the corners of her eyes. She owed him some sort of explanation for her presence here tonight. The last thing she wanted was for him to wonder at a later date if she'd been up to something fishy.

But she wasn't about to tell him that this whole hysterical fiasco had been caused by the chain letter he'd teased her about the other day. She did have some dignity left.

And if she had to lie to hold on to it, so be it. "I was looking for Liza's sketches," Beth murmured, averting her gaze. "She was working, and she . . . needed them."

"The sketches?" Chance stopped and turned to her, his expression apologetic. "Guilty as charged."

Beth's mouth dropped. "Excuse me?"

"I have them." He grinned and tapped the bottom of her chin with his index finger. "You'll catch flies. Hold on, they're on my desk."

Beth snapped her mouth shut and watched as he ducked back into his office. Chance had the sketches? She thought she'd had them, had thought them tucked safely into her portfolio. Hadn't she put them away the other day?

She couldn't remember.

Chance returned with the sketches and handed them to her. "Please apologize to Liza too. I forgot I had them."

Beth looked at the envelope, then back at him. She wanted to ask why he'd had them, wanted to so badly, the question burned on the tip of her tongue. Surely he knew she was curious, surely he could read the question in her eyes.

But he wasn't offering explanations.

Chance inclined his head. "Let's get out of here."

Swallowing the question and acknowledging her cowardice, Beth followed him, the envelope containing her sketches clutched in her hands. Without speaking, they crossed the lot to where their cars were parked side by side.

"Borrowed or new?" Chance asked as they stopped beside her compact wagon.

She fished for her keys. "It's all mine."

Chance looked down at her, studying the lines of her face. She lifted her eyes; their eyes met and held. Awareness eased up her spine. She called herself a fool.

"Well . . ." she murmured, clearing her throat.

"Well," Chance repeated, shoving his hands into his pockets. "It's been fun."

"Fun," she repeated, knowing his words meant nothing, but feeling them like a punch to her gut. How did he do it? she wondered. How could he make her feel awkward and aware and tingly all at once, and by doing nothing more than looking at her?

Chance plucked the keys from her fingers and opened the car door. She slid inside, anxious to put some distance between them.

He bent down and handed her the keys. "I guess this is good night."

"I guess it is," she murmured, her voice thick.

"Drive carefully."

"I will."

Still Chance didn't move. Beth swallowed, her mouth suddenly desert-dry. Dear Lord, she couldn't be thinking the kind of things about him that she was. Like how his lips would feel on hers, how his hands would move over her body.

But she was.

Pretty hot thoughts for the last surviving virgin in North America.

The time had come to go home. The faster the better. "Have a good weekend," she said quickly, sticking the key into the ignition.

She turned the key.

Nothing.

This couldn't be happening, she told herself, her hands beginning to shake. Even bad luck could only go so far. Taking a deep breath, she tried again.

Still nothing.

After trying several more times with no luck, Beth rested her forehead on the steering wheel. Well, she had to admit it, she was a cursed woman. And if the letter lived up to its "or else," she would be hit by a bus any moment now.

She looked up at Chance. "You'd better get out of here, I wouldn't want you to get hit by any of the debris."

"Debris?"

"From the accident. A bus is going to hit me. Wait, I think I hear one now."

Chance laughed and opened her car door. "Let me try."

She sighed. "If you knew the kind of day I've had, you would know it's useless. This car is not going to start."

"You never know."

"Okay, be an optimist." She shrugged and climbed out so he could climb in.

Chance tried the car with no more success than she. After a couple of minutes he slid back out. "We'll call you a tow, then I'll give you a ride home."

Beth made a sound of disgust and frustration and dropped her face into her hands. "I thought this night couldn't get any worse." She peeked at him over the tops of her fingers. "I was wrong. And right now I'd like to scream, I'm so mad."

"I'd say go ahead, but considering our evening, I'm afraid I might get arrested." Chance tipped his head and grinned. "But kicking a tire might do the trick. Nothing like an immature display of temper to get rid of frustration."

Beth eyed him, then the front tire. She wanted to do it, wanted to wheel back and nail that tire with everything she had. "You're convinced this will work?"

"Oh, yeah, let that hostility out. You'll be surprised how much better you'll feel." Chance folded his arms across his chest and rested against the side of the car. "You might want to swear while you do it, but that's optional."

"I think I will." Setting her jaw, Beth kicked the tire—so hard her toes stung and her eyes watered. She felt a hundred times better anyway.

Then she heard a hissing sound.

"Uh-oh."

Beth looked at Chance, then followed his gaze. The hissing sound was the air going out of the tire—at an extremely rapid rate. As they watched, the tire went pancake-flat.

Beth giggled. Her giggles became laughter; she laughed until she cried. Then she was in Chance's arms for the second time that night, weeping against his shoulder, soaking his shirt and feeling like a total ninny.

Chance held Beth as she sobbed, not having the faintest idea what to do. Weeping women were not his specialty. Not by a long shot.

"Don't cry," he said awkwardly, stroking her hair. "It'll be all right."

Face still pressed against his chest, Beth shook her head. "You don't understand . . . this has been a *really* bad day." She drew in a shuddering breath. "My goldfish died and my car died and my apartment was robbed. And now my new car's dead, too."

Chance breathed in the scent of her hair. It was sweet and fruity, like watermelon candy. "That *is* a bad day," he murmured, brushing his lips against the soft strands.

"And now I've made a fool of myself," she said, hiccuping.

"No." Chance tangled his fingers in the fiery strands of her hair. How could this woman feel so good in his arms? he wondered. Why did she feel so right?

He tipped her face up to his and gently smoothed

the tears from her cheeks. "Losing a goldfish can be a traumatic thing."

Her lips lifted. He felt the movement like a blow to his solar plexus. "Ah, Red . . ." Chance buried his fingers deeper in her hair, cupping the back of her head. "This is crazy."

"Yes," she murmured, swaying toward him, her eyes fluttering shut.

Even as he lowered his head to hers, he called himself a fool.

Her lips were wet and tasted salty from her tears. He kissed her lightly, ever so softly moving his mouth against hers. Her lips trembled, then softened and parted. Drinking her tears, Chance took what she so shyly offered.

Beth flattened her hands against Chance's chest. Through the soft cotton of his pullover, she felt the heat of his flesh and the thunder of his heart. All the bad luck in the world was worth this moment, she thought dizzily. She'd never been kissed this way, never reacted this way. She burned, she ached. She wanted.

She slid her hands to his shoulders. She didn't care what he felt or why he kissed her. She could do nothing but revel in this moment and the sensations flashing, lightninglike, through her body.

Curling her fingers around his shoulders, she deepened the kiss.

Chance groaned as her tongue shyly touched his. He reacted and responded, even as he acknowledged how inexperienced she was. He tightened his arms around her, bending her backward under the force of his kiss.

The dark enveloped them, the breeze gently buffeted. The buzz of distant traffic was replaced by the sound of his own blood pounding in his ears. And the small whimpering sounds that came from deep in her throat.

He wanted her. She wanted him. All he would have to do was say the word and she would be in his bed.

He had better run for his life.

The thoughts collided in his brain and Chance lifted his head. Her eyes were open, and she gazed at him with a combination of shock and desire and . . . trust.

Chance stiffened, moving a step away from her. He tried to smile. And failed. "I told you this was crazy," he said, his voice thick.

Beth looked at the ground. She'd lied to herself—she did care what he felt. She did care why he'd kissed her.

Chance swore silently. He'd hurt her. He saw it in the stiff way she held herself, the way she avoided meeting his gaze. Regret and remorse curled through him, and Chance lifted a hand to cup her cheek, then dropped it.

If she was angry, if she hated him even, it would be for the best. This was not a woman who dallied. This was not a woman who would think nothing of kisses shared under a dark, star-studded sky.

And he was a man who did and thought exactly that.

"Beth, I . . . I'm sorry. I just . . ." He groped for the right words, because the honest ones wouldn't do at all. "You were crying," he said finally, inadequately, "and I didn't know what else to do."

Hurt arced through her. And anger. The earth had moved, and he hadn't known what else to do. Classic.

Color climbed her cheeks, and Beth lifted her chin. "Sorry about putting you in that awkward position. Believe me, it won't happen again."

He swore again. Her eyes were blue pools of hurt. She hadn't the experience—or the guile—to conceal what she felt. "Dammit, Beth, I didn't—"

"It was *just* a kiss, Chance." She tossed her head back. "For Pete's sake, I am a grown-up. I *have* been kissed before."

He shoved his hands into his pockets, unreasonably annoyed by her words even as he told himself to be relieved. "This *has* been an unusual night."

"Exactly." Beth fought to keep her tone even and almost businesslike. "And since I doubt we'll ever be in this type of situation again—"

"It'll never happen again," he supplied, fighting the urge to take her back into his arms and kiss her silly. He turned toward his car. "Why don't I call that tow truck, then I'll give you a lift home."

A week later Beth stood outside Chance's office door, her heart a freight train in her chest. She had serious financial problems: no clothes, no furniture, no savings, only a piece-of-junk car.

Beth wiped her damp palms against her thighs. She could see only one viable solution—become Chance's personal assistant. She wanted the job, she had for a long time. She could do it, she knew she could.

All she had to do was convince Chance of that fact.

Chance. Beth squeezed her eyes shut, thinking of their kiss, reliving every nuance of the moment, her every sensation. She could still taste him, could still feel the pressure of his mouth on hers, feel the pounding of her pulse as she'd clung to him.

And she could still see the expression in his eyes as he'd pulled away from her. Disbelief. Regret. Anxiety.

Dammit. She had to put this thing into perspective; he obviously had. During the last week, he'd joked and teased and treated her as he always had—like his funny little receptionist.

And why shouldn't he? They'd shared only a kiss, after all. If he could handle that, so could she.

Taking a deep breath, Beth peeked into Chance's office. His head was bent as he flipped through some papers; his thick dark hair tumbled across his forehead in a way that made her want to smooth it back with gentle fingers.

She clasped her hands together. Thoughts like those did nothing to calm her nerves. Nor did remembering the brush of his mouth on hers or the feel of his heart beating under her palm.

Beth squeezed her eyes shut, shook her head, and took another deep breath. She was a grown woman, not an ingenue with a crush. She *could* do this.

Bold, she told herself, lifting her chin jauntily. Self-confident and determined.

With those thoughts ringing in her head, Beth stepped fully into Chance's doorway. "Chance, do you have a minute?"

He looked up and smiled. The curving of his lips was slow, sexy, and sanity-stealing. Her confidence slipped a notch, and she ordered herself to get a grip.

"For you? Of course." He motioned her in. "Have a seat."

Beth crossed the room and, choosing one of the two leather and chrome chairs across from his desk, sat down. She was still trying to remember all the words she'd practiced, the gestures and facial expressions that Eva had coached her on, when Chance suddenly spoke.

"Did you have a nice weekend?"

"Very nice. And you?"

"Good. Fine." He capped his pen and tossed it onto the papers littering his desk. "How's your car?"

Heat crept up her cheeks as the memory of that night flooded her mind. She cursed the telltale color and attempted a casual smile. "Fixed. Almost."

Silence fell between them. Clearing her throat, she tried again. "It's been two weeks and we haven't had any luck with our ad."

"That's an understatement." Chance tapped the stack of résumés in front of him. "The best applicant so far has an undergraduate degree in art, but no business skills and no arts management. And frankly, he acted like a flake."

Beth swallowed. Hard. She had no art degree and no arts management. She'd gotten her business degree only by the skin of her teeth. But she wasn't a flake. She thought of the way she'd swooned in his arms the other night and grimaced, uncertain Chance would agree with her assessment.

Chance pushed the hair away from his forehead. "Let's run the ad for another week," he continued. "You never know when the perfect person will walk through the door."

He'd just given her an out—she could leave now and he would never wonder why she'd knocked. But he'd also given her the perfect in. Screwing up her courage, Beth blurted, "She already has."

Chance lifted his eyebrows. "Excuse me?"

"The perfect person . . . through that door. Me." When he still didn't seem to understand, she added, "I'd like to be your assistant. I'd like the job."

Beth could see that she'd surprised him. She didn't find the fact comforting. "I've wanted it all along," she rushed on. "Each time one of your assistants quit, I'd hoped you'd think of me."

"I see." Chance leaned back in his chair. "So, now you've taken matters into your own hands."

"Yes."

"Beth, you're a valued employee. I want you to understand that. But I'm not sure about this. As evidenced by the number of assistants that come and go around here, I'm difficult to deal with."

"I know that."

"Do you?" He picked the pen back up and tapped it thoughtfully against the desk top. "I'm demanding to the point of tyranny, honest to the point of rude. I don't watch my tongue and I don't pull punches. And you seem . . . sensitive."

Beth knew exactly what he referred to—the other night and her tears. She clasped her hands tighter in her lap and refused to retreat. "Your badgering will not scare me off. In the last six months I've taken plenty of it and haven't run home in tears. The circumstances of the other night were . . . special."

"Yes," Chance murmured, moving his gaze slowly over her face. "They were."

His gaze found hers; she couldn't look away.

Chance broke the contact first. "Do the police have any leads?"

"No." Her voice sounded husky even to her own ears, and she prayed Chance wouldn't notice. "They told me they probably wouldn't."

"I'm sorry."

"It's okay. I'm dealing with it." Beth looked down at her hands, then back up at him. "I think I can do the job, Chance. I know I want to try . . ."

Beth let her words trail off at the reticence in his expression, her resolve evaporating. *He* didn't think she could do it. That was obvious. Maybe she was the one being unrealistic. Maybe she should back off, admit she—

No. She curled her fingers into fists. For the first time in her life she wasn't going to be ruled by insecurity, by fears or what ifs. For the first time in her life she was going to express how she felt and what she wanted.

Beth straightened her spine. "Let me amend that. I *know* I can do the job. I'm smart and a hard worker. I already know Art One procedures. I know the artists, the clients and gallery directors. They all like me."

Beth marveled at the clarity and confidence in her voice. Giddy with a feeling of power, she stood and faced him. "I want this job, Chance. Give me the opportunity to prove to you that I can do it."

Chance rubbed the side of his jaw thoughtfully, buying time. Everything she said was true. He'd received many compliments on her performance since she'd started at Art One. She was efficient and punctual and hardworking. She took the initiative and did more than required in her job description.

But still . . . Chance swung his chair around toward the window and stared out at the brilliant day. He thought of how she'd looked that morning, standing hesitantly in his doorway, looking at once determined and as though she wanted to run for her life. The rush of warmth he'd felt for her in that moment had startled him. As had the pleasure he'd experienced at just looking at her.

He'd fought them off, just as he'd fought the memory of their kiss. She'd affected him like a spark to explosives; he couldn't remember when the simple brush of mouth to mouth had made him feel so much. Or so strongly. If it ever had at all.

Explosions blew worlds apart and forced reasonable men into unreasonable acts. Acts they would come to bitterly regret, acts that wounded innocent parties. Chance understood that. His own father and mother had taught by example.

Chance frowned. And none of that had a thing to do with the decision Beth was asking him to make now.

It had taken a lot for her to face him, to ask for the job. He knew her well enough to know that. She wanted it badly. More than any of the assistants he'd ever hired, certainly more than the lame ducks he'd interviewed in the last couple of weeks.

Chance thought of the expression in her eyes and voice when she'd talked of her sister's artwork. She had passion for art. She understood it. She loved it.

Sunlight tumbled through the windows, creating bright patches of light on the floor and walls, on himself. He put his hand over one of the bright rectangles. He stared at the shape of light, its warmth penetrating his skin. Beth Waters's eyes were as guileless as a sunny day; she smelled of sunshine. When he looked at her, he thought of spring.

Chance swung back around. She stood still as a stone, her expression a combination of hope, determination, and apprehension. He didn't like that the combination tugged at him. Emotionalism had no place in business, no place in his relationships with his assistants.

Or in any of his other relationships.

"What about the job you do now?" he asked, his voice brusque.

"I'll call an agency," Beth said quickly. "We'll have somebody by noon."

Still he didn't commit. Heart hammering against the wall of her chest, Beth placed her palms on his desk and leaned toward him. "Give me two months. A trial period. If it doesn't work out, I'm back at the receptionist's desk. No complaints. No pouting or hysterics. I want this job. I need it. Give me the chance to prove I can do it."

Chance grinned; he couldn't help himself. His little mouse had turned into a lion. He'd known a lot of high-powered, gusty women, but at this moment they had nothing on Beth Waters.

She was right too. A trial period offered him a no-lose scenario. It offered him a solution to his immediate problem and offered her an opportunity to prove herself. And both of them an easy out if the solution didn't work.

"I'm still skeptical," he murmured.

"I've got the job?"

"Two months. Start first thing in the morning."

She laughed out loud, delighted. She felt brave and powerful, able to conquer the world. For the first time in her life she'd gone after what she wanted— and she'd gotten it!

"You won't regret this," she said, practically skipping to the door.

Chance watched her, amused—and charmed—by her delight. He couldn't remember ever having made anyone quite so happy. It felt good.

"No," he said softly, "I don't think I will."

Beth paused at the door. "I'll call an agency immediately."

"You do that." He grinned. "And be ready to kick butt tomorrow morning. You know I will."

Four

"What do you mean you can't find it?" Chance demanded, propping the phone into the crook between his neck and shoulder and waving Beth into his office. "Dammit, Cody, buildings don't just get up and walk away!"

Beth's heart sank. This was the first time she'd been late in the two weeks since she and Chance had begun their trial period—and it looked as though her timing had been bad in more ways than one.

Chance covered the mouthpiece with his hand. "Where the hell have you been? This is the sixth call about—" He swung his attention back to what the caller was saying. "Yes, dammit, I do think a map would be a good idea."

Beth shoved her paint-stained hands into her pockets. She'd gotten up at four A.M., consumed by the need to work on a problematic painting, and even the alarm she'd set hadn't roused her from her art. She had a rule about not painting before work for precisely that reason.

"Call me back."

Just as Chance replaced the receiver, the phone rang again. Not waiting for the receptionist, Beth grabbed it. "Art One." As she spoke to the caller, she held up a finger to indicate to Chance that she needed to talk with him and that he should wait. He scowled at her.

"Yes, Joe?" Beth listened to the man on the other end of the line, understanding immediately Chance's call of a moment ago. Today an important installation was going up at World Life. She'd spent the last two weeks coordinating every detail of the event, including getting maps made for the drivers. Unfortunately, the directions she'd gotten from World's curator led not to the insurance company's swank new corporate offices but to a taco stand in East L.A.

"You're sure you didn't miss an exit or . . . Okay, okay." Beth plucked the pen from Chance's desk set. "What's the number there? Stay put, I'll get back to you.

"The maps are wrong," she said calmly, picking the phone back up and dialing World Life. "This isn't a big deal."

Chance stopped pacing. "Twenty technicians on hand, being paid by the hour to install works that are God knows where, and she tells me this isn't a big deal."

"Calm down. We know where they are or are heading—Fat Maria's Taco Hut." He didn't laugh, and she rolled her eyes and punched out World's number. "If any of the other drivers call in, get a number and tell them to stand by."

Chance whirled around and glowered at her. Beth smiled and got the switchboard to connect her with the curator at World.

Within minutes she had an apology, revised directions, and the promise that things would be smoothed over on that end. One by one the drivers called in, received the new directions, and got back on their way.

"There," Beth said crisply, turning back to Chance. "Crisis over. And we lost only a couple of hours."

"The Art One wizard does it again." Smiling, he shook his head. "You amaze me."

She waved aside his praise. "I just made a phone call."

"And managed to soothe the savage breast. And everybody along the way."

Beth smiled shyly, coloring with pleasure. "It was nothing."

"It was something. The owner of the savage breast, by the way, apologizes for being so—"

"Savage," she supplied, then laughed. "Don't worry about it. After all, you have your reputation to think of."

"Unreasonable bastard."

Beth angled him an amused glance. "That's the one."

His eyebrows shot up in mock outrage. "You're getting pretty cheeky, Ms. Waters. Perhaps I better buy you a cup of coffee."

Suddenly tongue-tied, Beth nodded, and together they walked to the kitchen. Working alongside Chance the last couple of weeks had been a mixed blessing. On the one hand, she loved the work. It challenged her, excited her. It was fun. But on the other, being with Chance day in and day out, having their hands brush, their gazes meet in silent communication, laughing and talking together, had been an agony.

She wanted them to be more than employer, employee. She wanted them to be more than friends.

She wanted the impossible.

"Car trouble again?" Chance asked, referring, she

knew, to her tardiness. He filled two cups and handed her one.

She took the cup, conscious of the paint stains on her fingers. "No," she murmured vaguely, "I just got . . . involved with something."

Chance leaned against the counter and studied her over the rim of his coffee cup. Seconds ticked past, and Beth shifted nervously.

"What?" she asked finally, smoothing her khaki-colored skirt.

Chance shrugged and sipped. "You're odd."

"Odd?" she squeaked.

He smiled. "Maybe odd's not quite the right description. Unusual's better."

"Oh, much better," she said. She likened him to Michelangelo's *David*, and he thought of her as . . . unusual. "Maybe you could think of me as unusually odd."

"There you go," he said, laughing. "Your cheeks are the color of fire, but your wit is immediate and acerbic. One moment you're shy, the next bold. You're timid and easily embarrassed, but calm in a crisis and levelheaded, even with the most unreasonable clients."

"Or bosses."

"Right." Chance leaned toward her conspiratorially. "Just how many of you are there?"

Beth thought of Liza and wanted to cringe. If he only knew. "Just call me Sybil."

He shook his head, amused. "You make me laugh."

It could be worse, she thought. She could make him sick.

"Where do you come from, Beth Waters?" he asked. "I know little about you except that you have an eccentric grandmother and an equally eccentric sister. What's the rest of your family like? Totally insane?"

Beth turned away from him on the pretense of adding more cream to her coffee. "Actually," she said softly and after a moment, "the rest of my family is quite sane. Bland as bathwater, in fact. They pride themselves on being just like the people next door. Middle-class values and lifestyle—brick ranch house in the 'burbs, shaggy dog, and a station wagon. My father's an accountant, my mother a homemaker."

"Intriguing," Chance teased, leaning against the counter and propping his chin on his fist. "Tell me more."

Beth shrugged. "There's not much else to tell. My parents rewarded levelheadedness. Expected it, really. Tantrums weren't allowed. Outbursts of any sort were discouraged." She stirred her coffee, still avoiding his gaze. "Normalcy was encouraged. As was moderation in all things."

She finally turned to face him. "That's probably why I don't mind my crazy neighbor—I can't get much farther from Kansas than Mrs. Beaver."

A sadness slipped over her expression, and Chance frowned. He reached out and trailed his index finger over the curve of her cheek. Her skin was as soft as satin, and warm and pliant. His pulse stirred. "What are you thinking?"

She shifted her gaze. "About how much my parents could say without even uttering a sound."

Chance gave in to the urge and cupped her face in his palm. "And what did they say to you without words?"

Beth ached at the memory of the things her parents hadn't said about her art. About her. "How much I disappointed them."

Chance felt her words like a punch to his gut and

fought the impulse to take her into his arms. Instead he brushed his thumb slowly, rhythmically across her cheekbone. His breath caught as she tipped her face into the caress.

That simple and trusting gesture affected him more than any of his own physical sensations, and the truth of that had him reeling. He dropped his hand.

"I think," he said, his voice thick, "I would have liked your generic little ranch house. My parents were both artists. I learned early that art supplies came before milk or new school shoes or birthday parties. In my parents' home, what hung on the walls was so much more important than the walls themselves, a canvas or drawing always took precedent over a couch or chair. And they were temperamental."

"So that's where you get it," Beth murmured, feeling bereft without his touch, wishing that he would touch her again.

Chance smiled softly but without amusement. "Tantrums, outbursts, and hurt feelings were the order of the day. In fact, our lives were one bloody battle after another. They divorced when I was thirteen."

"I'm sorry."

"Don't be. It was better for them, although I can't say that our lives became any less tumultuous—the emotional focus just shifted."

Surprised at himself, Chance shook off the memories and their corresponding emotions. He'd never shared that part of himself with another, had never felt the need to. But in those moments, he had wanted her to understand him. It had seemed so natural, so right, to share himself with her.

Unnerved, he forced a casual smile. "Things work out. I got my love of art from them."

"But you didn't want to be an artist yourself?" she asked, her voice husky with emotion.

"Didn't have the gift or the drive." He took a sip of his cold coffee and grimaced. Crossing to the sink, he dumped it and rinsed the cup.

When he swung back around, all traces of melancholy were gone from his expression. "So tell me, how did your sister fare in this oh-so-normal household?"

"My sister?"

"You have more than one?"

"No." Beth lowered her eyes. Tell him now, she thought. Get out of this fabrication before it's too late. Explain that she had been embarrassed, insecure about her art and . . .

But what if he didn't understand? What if he fired her?

The thought of losing her job made her ache; the thought of Chance thinking less of her scared her. As much as she hated lying to him, she couldn't face the consequences of the truth.

If she couldn't come clean about Liza, at least she could speak from her heart. "She fared the same as I—as best she could. They never understood her need to create, never thought she had any talent. They made it plain they thought she would fall flat on her face."

"And has she?"

Beth felt the color drain from her cheeks. She opened her mouth to answer, then shut it again as Jody, the new receptionist, stuck her head into the kitchen. "Problem at the install. Something about a piece not fitting in its designated space."

"I'll take care of it," Beth said quickly, dumping the

last of her coffee in the sink and starting out of the kitchen.

"Beth?"

She paused and looked back at him.

"Tell her for me, I don't think she has."

Beth's heart stopped, then started again with a vengeance. "Thanks," she murmured, the word catching in her throat. "I will." Not trusting herself to say anything more, she hurried for the phone.

It was nearly noon before Beth came up for air. The install was finally on smooth footing; even the curator sounded happy.

Only then did Beth remember her lunch date with Eva. She checked her watch and swore silently. Today was not the day to leave the office for a leisurely lunch. She picked up the phone to catch her grandmother before she left, then swore again when she got her machine.

"Problem?"

Beth hung up the phone and looked up. Chance stood in her doorway. "I just remembered I promised Eva I'd go to lunch with her today."

He sauntered across to her desk. "So go."

"But the install—"

"Isn't everything under control?"

"Well, yes . . ." Beth tapped her chin with her index finger. "But I hate to leave when—"

Chance caught her hand, inspecting her stained fingers. He rubbed them gently, then brought her hand to his nose. He met her eyes. "You've been playing in paint, Ms. Waters. Oil paint."

Beth's heart began to hammer. She slipped her hand from his, dropping it to her lap. "I stopped by Liza's studio on the way in—she's back in town—and we got to talking and . . . I helped her clean up." Beth cleared her throat. "Let me try Eva again."

Chance took the receiver from her hand and dropped it back into its cradle. "You deserve a lunch out. I want you to go."

"But—"

"No buts. You're going." He settled himself on the edge of her desk, picked up a framed photo of her and Eva, studied it for a moment, then set it back down. "Speaking of going, have you ever been to the Artful Fools Ball?"

"Artful Fools," she repeated. An extravaganza put on to benefit the South Orange County Cultural Center and Foundation, Artful Fools was held on April Fools' Day and was considered the zaniest event of the year. Eva had been a couple of times, and although Beth had always wanted to go, she'd never been able to afford it.

Beth shook her head in answer. "Why?"

"Because I have two tickets and wondered if you would like to go."

"With you?"

"None other."

"Oh."

He reached out and gently lifted her chin. "I hope that's a yes?"

"Yes. I mean, I'd love to go."

"Good." He stood. "A number of collectors will be there, many of our artists attend. The press will be in attendance—really, everyone who's anyone in the L.A. art community. It'll be a terrific opportunity for you to meet people."

A sliver of disappointment speared through her, and she fought it off. For a moment she had allowed herself to hope he'd asked her for a reason other than business. "Sounds perfectly terrifying."

Chance laughed. "Don't worry, Red, I won't just throw you to the wolves." He crossed to the door, stopping and turning back to her when he reached it. "Saturday night. Dress is formal. I'll pick you up at seven."

"Formal?" she repeated. Today was Thursday. Where in the world would she find a dress by Saturday? And how would she pay for it?

"Is that going to be a problem?"

Beth looked up at Chance and shook her head. "No problem. If I have to, I'll just borrow something."

"From Liza?"

Beth inched her chin up, unreasonably annoyed that he thought Liza would have a dress when she herself obviously didn't. "Eva, probably."

"Great."

After flashing her a quick smile, Chance ducked out of her office.

Chance paused outside Beth's apartment door. He wasn't nervous, he told himself. He certainly wasn't excited. Tonight was business and nothing more.

Sure. The thoughts he'd been having all day—ones of Beth in his arms, soft and yielding, of her mouth on his, open and inviting—were the result of . . .

Chance frowned, searching for a plausible reason. He swore silently when he didn't come up with anything. This had to stop. Beth Waters was not for him. She was a serious kind of woman, a woman who expected commitments—like marriage and children. He was the kind of man who ran from commitments.

Annoyed with his own thoughts, Chance knocked on her door. A person always wanted what he couldn't have. It was human nature; he was no exception. Beth Waters was off-limits, which made her more attractive, more alluring, more—

Chance's thoughts came to an abrupt halt as she swung the door open. Stunned, he moved his gaze slowly over her. Her dress revealed nothing but hinted at everything. Unrelieved black, it skimmed over her curves, teasing, daring a man to touch, to explore, to discover for himself.

He let out a husky "Wow."

She tried to smile and failed. The heat in her cheeks became fire, and she ran a hand self-consciously over her hip. "Do I . . . look all right?"

"All right doesn't even start to cover it. You look sensational."

"You really think so?" She smiled with pleasure, reaching up and nervously touching her hair, which she had piled on top of her head. "I'll grab my wrap."

She swung around; Chance made a strangled sound of disbelief. The dress had no back. None. From the big rhinestone button at her nape to the small of her back—and beyond—the dress had been cut away to reveal and tempt. Her white skin glowed in shocking contrast to the ebony of the dress.

Arousal swept over him, and he simultaneously thanked and cursed the sadistic designer who had fashioned her gown.

Beth turned back to him, her expression alarmed. "I borrowed it from Eva . . . it was the most demure she had." Beth looked down at herself. "It's too much, isn't it?"

Chance coughed. "It is," he managed, his voice thick, "but that's what makes it so . . . wow."

She wasn't quite sure how to take that, and caught her bottom lip between her teeth. "You're certain?"

Chance laughed, charmed and refreshed by her honesty. The women he usually dated never doubted their looks. And even if they did, they would never admit it.

Of course, he reminded himself, this wasn't a date.

"I'm certain. In fact, you'll no doubt be the hit of the party. I'll have to fight off armies of suitors. I'll probably have to slay a dragon, or King Kong, or—"

Laughing, Beth cut him off. "Okay, already. I'll get my wrap."

Her wrap consisted of an outrageously long black-and-white chiffon scarf. Chance helped her drape it around her shoulders, and they stepped out into the night.

The trip from her apartment to the Cultural Center took nearly an hour. Chance drove at a leisurely pace, more interested in studying Beth than in getting to the party.

She continued to intrigue him. She was a woman of contrasts, at one moment painfully shy, the next witty; she could be reserved and timid, yet when she laughed, she held nothing back. She had no self-confidence when it came to her looks, yet she could handle the most arrogant and demanding collectors with an ease that astounded him. Who was this woman?

For about the twentieth time since they'd left her apartment, he glanced at her from the corners of his eyes. She stared straight ahead, her hands clasped tightly in her lap, her back stiff. She looked as if she were preparing herself for the electric chair. He reached across and covered her hands with one of his own. "Don't be nervous."

"How did you know?"

"Even in the dark I can see your fingers turning white from lack of circulation. They're cold." He rubbed his fingers against hers, warming them. "Relax, Beth. I won't let anybody bite."

"Darn, that'll take all the fun out of it."

He laughed, then growled softly. "I won't let anybody else bite, that is." She blushed and lowered her eyes; he laughed again. "Don't worry, even in that dress you're safe."

That was exactly what worried her. The last thing she wanted to be was safe. Disappointment curled through her, but she met his gaze evenly. "I'm not a complete innocent, you know."

Chance thought of that night in the parking lot, thought of the way she'd melted against him. There had been nothing innocent about their kiss, nor about the way she'd responded to it. "No," he murmured. "I know."

He squeezed her hand, then released it so he could turn into the Center's parking lot. "I think I'd better warn you about this party . . . it gets a little weird."

"Weird?" she repeated, nervous again. "You don't mean anything illegal or—"

"Immoral?" He laughed. "No, nothing like that. But if someone comes up to you and starts talking in pig Latin, play along."

Someone did, indeed, come up and talk to her in pig Latin. Luckily, pig Latin had been the one foreign language she'd excelled at in school. Amused, Chance listened to her converse with the gentleman—one of the foundation's board members and the evening's host.

The building that housed the Cultural Center had been the home of one of California's wealthiest citizens. An art patron, he had donated the building and property to the foundation more than a dozen years back. The ten-thousand-square-foot building, designed and built by architect Frank Lloyd Wright, was nestled into the side of a cliff overlooking the ocean and was considered an architectural gem.

Beth had always wanted to see the inside, but she would have to wait a bit longer to see it in its normal state. Because tonight the Cultural Center had been transformed into a fantasy world of magical colors, shapes, textures, and sounds, a world where art, interior, and inhabitant became one.

Stunned, Beth dragged her gaze from the surreal vision before her to look at Chance. At her expression, he laughed. "It's a long way from Kansas, isn't it?"

"But not far at all from Oz."

Chance smiled and tucked her arm through his. "Come, let's mingle."

They moved through the sea of people, many of them costumed, some even masked. The costumes ranged from merely elaborate to outlandish beyond description. Beth spotted some traditional figures: Marie Antoinette, Napoleon Bonaparte, Vincent van Gogh; and some less traditional: the California Raisins, a Mayan god, figures from Picasso's first cubist masterpiece, *Les Demoiselles d'Avignon*.

Beth grinned up at Chance. "Have you ever costumed?"

He returned her grin. "Last year I came as Zoro."

Picturing him as the masked man, Beth laughed and let him lead her around the room. He introduced her to one person after another, keeping his word and never leaving her side.

They laughed and danced and drank champagne. The wine was fine and dry; the bubbles went straight to her head. Even so, she let the circling waiters replace her empty glasses with full ones.

Beth and Chance talked to Eva and her date, an artist twenty-five years her junior. Everyone knew Chance, and he introduced her as his irreplaceable new assistant. Even introduced as a business associate, Beth was leveled with some speculative stares, especially from women. Rather than self-conscious, the assessing looks made her feel proprietary. Even possessive.

Tonight Chance was hers.

As the minutes passed, Beth became more aware of Chance at her side, of his warmth and his strength, of the feel of his fingers on her naked back when he would silently steer her toward a new group, of the feel of his breath against her ear when he would whisper something to her, of the husky quality of his voice when he would say words of amusement.

"Are you hungry?" Chance asked.

"Starved." She tipped her head back and laughed up at him. "I was too excited to eat today."

He moved his gaze slowly over her flushed face. "I think you've had too much champagne."

Beth laughed again. She wished she could blame the wine for her light-headedness, but she knew the wine had little to do with it. "You can never have too much champagne, didn't you know? It's a law of nature."

Chance lifted his eyebrows, amused. "I know another law of nature, one about drinking on an empty stomach. Come on." He laced his fingers with hers and led her to the buffet.

The rest of the guests had lost interest in the food and had gone on to wilder pursuits, leaving Beth and Chance to themselves and the feast.

"What are all these things?" Beth asked, breathing deeply through her nose. "They smell heavenly."

"Heavenly," Chance murmured, his eyes on her rather than the display of exotic hors d'oeuvres. Her skin was as white as cream and looked as soft as silk. He let his gaze linger on the flesh exposed by her outrageous dress, taking in the delicate bones of her shoulders and back.

He shook his head and dragged his gaze away. He

selected a canapé from the assortment and held it to her mouth. She bit into it and made a sound of pleasure. His body tightened, and he swore silently. On the pretense of getting her a plate, he swung away from her.

What the hell was he doing? he wondered, selecting a variety of the finger foods for her to sample. Why, when it came to this woman, couldn't he do what he knew he must? Why couldn't he keep his distance?

He turned back to her, finding that she had crossed to the wall of glass that faced the ocean. A hundred feet below, the ocean crashed against the shore.

He set the plate aside and moved up behind her, acknowledging that he didn't know why. And that, for tonight, he wouldn't try to analyze, wouldn't question.

"It's dizzying," she murmured, not taking her gaze from the view.

Lightly touching her shoulders, Chance leaned toward her, inhaling in the fresh, light scent of her hair. "Would you like to go out?"

She tipped her head back, her eyes glowing sapphire in the soft light. "Could we?"

"Come." He took her hand and led her out a side door and down a curving flight of stairs. The stairs led to a small terrace cut into the side of the cliff.

The wind buffeted them, whipping her gown, tearing her hair from the pins anchoring it in place. The smell of the ocean was so strong, she grew drunk on it; the sound of the water roared in her ears, competing only with the thrum of her own blood.

Beth threw her arms out and her head back, and laughed up at the star-studded sky. "I love this!" She whirled around, arms still wide, face still turned to the heavens. "It's wonderful, exhilarating. Delicious."

Chance laughed with her, stunned at her daring, captivated by her uncomplicated beauty. "The first time I came out here I felt drunk, although I hadn't had a drop to drink. I felt at once large and small, a conqueror and the conquered."

"Yes. That's how I feel." Beth laughed again and crossed to the railing. She leaned over, breathing in the ocean, absorbing its power. At that moment she felt more alive, more free, than she had in her entire life. The wind caught in her hair, tugging more strands free. She pushed them away from her face and leaned farther out.

Chance caught her from behind, anchoring her to him with his arms around her waist. "You'll fall."

Laughing, she looked back at him. "But what a fall it would be."

He tightened his arms, his heart a drum in his chest. "I'd never forgive myself."

She turned in his arms. "Would you even miss me, Chance Michaels?"

He took in the wild color in her cheeks, the sparkle in her eyes, the rose of her mouth. He would miss her more than he should, in ways he would have thought impossible mere weeks ago. A lump formed in his throat and he swallowed against it. "Yes," he murmured. "I would miss you."

She stood on tiptoes and pressed her mouth to his, then spun away from him. "I fantasized about dancing under a sky just like this one."

"Did you?" he asked, closing the distance between them once again, drawing her against his chest. Even in the dark he could see her blush.

"I don't get out much." She pressed her hands to his chest. "You can probably tell."

"I find that hard to believe." Chance wrapped a

piece of her fiery, shiny hair around his finger. He brought it to his nose. The ocean hadn't stolen her own sweet scent, but combined with it to create something at once feminine and wild.

"You're so beautiful tonight." He lowered his eyes to her mouth. "So beautiful."

Beth sobered, the laughter dying on her lips. She shook her head. "I've never been beautiful. Never been . . . alluring."

"No?" Chance slipped his hands from her shoulders to the small of her back, then beyond, to softer curves and slight dimples, to the place where her dress disappointed by covering her once more.

"You are so alluring," he murmured, catching her bottom lip between his teeth and nipping. "So exciting." He pressed closer, moving his pelvis against hers, letting her know without words just how exciting she was.

"You"—he moved his lips to her ear, to the pulse that beat wildly just behind it—"are driving me mad with need."

Beth moaned and leaned into him, slipping her fingers beneath his tuxedo jacket to stroke the crisp white linen stretched across his broad chest, wishing it was his skin she stroked, not fabric.

She acknowledged that she'd had too much champagne. She acknowledged that tomorrow she would be overwhelmed by regrets and embarrassment. But none of that mattered at the moment. All that mattered were Chance's arms, his touch, that he wanted her.

Beth pressed herself against him. "Then kiss me, Chance. Show me the way I make you feel."

With a groan, Chance did as she asked. Her lips were moist and already parted; she tasted of the fruity wine, of the delicately seasoned canapés, of desire.

Who was this woman? he wondered, twining his tongue with hers, sampling all the secrets of her mouth. Shy virgin or exotic temptress? He didn't know anymore.

He'd thought Beth Waters plain, now he thought her quietly alluring. He'd thought her conservative, he now considered her subtle. He'd thought her shy, he knew now she had great passion, a well of fire as hot as the color of her hair.

She moaned low in her throat and he pressed closer, desire speeding over him, his arousal painful. He moved his hands in slow circles against the small of her back, then dripped his fingers underneath the fabric to stroke whiter skin, skin that had never been kissed by the sun.

Chance dragged his mouth from hers, to taste her ear, her throat, her shoulder. "Beth . . . Beth . . ."

In response to his words, Beth arched against him. He made her feel beautiful. He made her feel sexy, made her feel for the first time like a whole woman.

Places that had never wanted, ached for his touch; places that had never been touched, warmed, then grew damp. And those feelings made her daring enough to act on her needs. And to hope. Murmuring his name, she dragged his mouth back to hers.

A woman like Beth would always draw a man back, Chance thought, reality crashing into him with the same force that the waves below struck the shore. And like the sand on that shore, he would be towed in and under.

He broke the kiss. She whimpered, and he twined his fingers in her hair, wanting to make love to her, wanting so badly he ached. She would acquiesce, he knew. She told him with her hungry eyes, with the way she clung to him. But she didn't play games; she was a woman without wiles. He would hurt her.

She wasn't for him.

"We should go in," he murmured, his voice thick with wanting.

"Must we?" she asked.

She trembled; the involuntary show of hurt tore at him. "Yes." With a gentleness that surprised him, he pushed the hair away from her face. "People will wonder."

Beth lowered her eyes. She wanted to tell him to let them. She wanted to suggest they make love. But she read the resignation—and the regret—in his eyes already. It was better that they end this now, before either of their regrets made it impossible for them to work together.

She forced a smile. "I've had too much wine."

Chance searched her expression and saw that the smile didn't quite reach her eyes. She was offering him an out. A better man would refuse it and pull her back into his arms. But he was who he was; he'd made his plans and promises long ago.

He brushed his mouth lightly against hers, then laced their fingers. Without speaking they climbed the stairs, parting at the top to go in search of mirrors to repair the damage made by the wind and their passion.

They met again by the dessert buffet. Chance held out a cup of coffee, and she took it with a weak smile of thanks. The vulnerable quality of her smile tore at him. He moved his gaze over her face, wanting to murmur soft words about what had occurred between them only minutes ago, but knowing some things must be left unsaid.

He felt both coward and fraud.

"There was no fixing my hair," she said, needing to fill the silence between them. "The . . . wind took too many of the pins."

Not the wind, Chance thought. His fingers. And his urgency. Frustration tightened in his chest, along with something else, something that made him ache. Chance reached out and touched her fiery mane of hair, just once and lightly, then dropped his hand. "I like it this way. It's—"

"My darlings, where *have* you been?" Eva swept across the room to where they stood, her date trailing behind her. She stopped and moved her gaze speculatively over them. "Well, well . . ."

Chance shifted and cleared his throat; Beth glowered at Eva, then turned and smiled at her grandmother's date. "Are you two having fun?"

Eva answered for him. "A delightful time, delicious, really."

The older woman batted her false eyelashes at Chance, and Beth ground her teeth. Really, she fumed, flirting with a man half her age.

Eva turned her attention to Beth, sweeping her gaze over her. The older woman narrowed her eyes, and Beth muttered an oath. Nothing slipped by her grandmother, and as soon as Eva got her alone, she would be in for the third degree.

If she even waited until she got her alone, Beth thought, a sinking sensation in the pit of her stomach. The sparkle in her grandmother's eyes was undeniable. And dangerous.

"*Grandmother*," Beth murmured, knowing the older woman hated the title, "aren't you and Raphael going to the art auction? I think it's about to start."

Eva ignored her and turned to Chance. "It's such a

shame Liza couldn't come. Then we'd all have been here."

Beth had told Eva all about the fiasco with the sketches and how her little fib had grown into a monster. She shot her grandmother a warning glance, not that she had much hope it would do any good.

Chance faced Beth. "How was the south of France, anyway? Did Liza enjoy her trip?"

Beth caught her bottom lip between her teeth. "Yes . . . I guess. We haven't talked much about it. Her trip, that is."

"It was marvelous," Eva cut in. "Liza is such an inspiration. So creative . . . so free. Whatever the whim, she follows it."

"Raphael, isn't one of your paintings being auctioned tonight?"

"You must meet her," the older woman continued as if Beth hadn't spoken. "And soon. She's absolutely delightful. You did know she's an artist?" Eva asked with exaggerated innocence. "Her work is nothing short of fabulous."

"I have wanted to meet her," Chance said. "I saw some of her sketches, and they looked interesting."

Listening to her grandmother sing Liza's praises and watching Chance hang on every word, Beth experienced a stab of jealousy, then groaned silently. Dear Lord, now she was competing with a sister she didn't even have.

"Beth, dear," her grandmother said, turning to her, "when are you going to get these two together? Liza is in town. You even said you thought Chance should take a look at her work."

Beth wanted to sink into the floor; she also wanted to wring her grandmother's neck. Instead she narrowed her eyes. "Have you forgotten, *Grandmother*, that she's leaving for—"

"Marrakesh," Eva cut in. "I just spoke with her, the trip's been canceled. She'll be here for the next . . . three months."

Chance looked at Beth. Eva looked at Beth. Beth decided the floor wasn't deep enough to sink into.

Beth took a steadying breath. She'd been cornered. Neatly too. Promising herself that she would never speak to her grandmother again, she forced a smile. "Well, if that's the case, I'll have to set something up."

"I'll look forward to it." Chance cocked his head. "I think you're right, Beth. The auction's started."

"Why don't you two go ahead," Beth said to the two men. "Eva and I need to talk for a moment. We'll meet you out there."

The moment Chance was out of earshot, Beth whirled on her grandmother. "How could you? How . . . could you?"

"I did it for your own good," Eva said primly, adjusting the spray of feathers at her hip. "You wouldn't show Chance your art, so Liza will."

Beth dropped her head into her hands, so furious she shook. After a moment she looked back up at the older woman. "Grandmother," she said softly, enunciating carefully, "I don't have a sister. There is no Liza. We both know this."

"Nonsense." Eva took out her compact and inspected her nose. "I've called you Liza all your life."

Beth sighed. "My grandmother's succumbed to senility, and my boss wants to meet my nonexistent sister. This is perfect." Beth sighed and closed her eyes. "What am I going to do now?"

"Senile, indeed. I resent that remark." Eva snapped the compact closed. "And the answer to your question is so simple. And so obvious."

Beth stiffened her spine. "Is that so? Well, why don't you fill me in, because at this moment nothing seems simple or obvious to me."

Her grandmother turned regally toward her. "My darling, you just become . . . Liza."

Five

For Beth the rest of the night passed in a disturbing blur. Now, ensconced in the dark of Chance's car, with him silent and brooding beside her, she could do nothing but think about the past hours and what had occurred between them. And wonder what she was going to do.

Beth turned and gazed out the car window. The night had started out so magically—they'd both been relaxed, they'd laughed and talked and enjoyed each other's company. Their embrace had changed that. From the moment they'd returned from the terrace, it had been awkward and uncomfortable between them.

Beth couldn't forget their passion, and she knew he couldn't either. For very different reasons.

She balled her fingers into fists in her lap. It hurt, knowing he regretted, knowing he would change those minutes if he had the ability to. Because, even though she ached—with embarrassment, with hurt—she wouldn't change one moment of that time on the terrace. Those moments had been the most special of her life.

Beth peeked at Chance from the corners of her eyes, her heart turning over as she found him studying her. Without acknowledging his gaze, she shifted hers back to the car window and the black night beyond. She sighed. How could Eva have chosen that moment to complicate her life even more?

Become Liza? Beth thought incredulously. The idea was ridiculous, and yet . . .

Beth shook her head, a feeling of panic tightening in her stomach. She could still hear her grandmother saying, "What are your other options, Liza dear? Getting fired? Running back to Kansas?"

And hearing "We told you so," Beth thought, twisting her fingers together in her lap. Admitting she had fallen flat on her face. Beth squeezed her eyes shut and sighed again. What was she going to do?

Chance heard Beth sigh and tightened his fingers on the steering wheel. He felt like a cad, a heel. Even knowing she wasn't the woman for him, even knowing she was inexperienced, he had kissed her. Chance scowled. What had occurred between them had been so much more than a kiss.

He wanted her still. So much so, the need clawed at him. But it would be wrong between them, he knew that. He could never give her anything more than sex. And hurt. That was the kind of man he was.

He stole a glance at her. What was she thinking? She had been uncommunicative since returning from the terrace, the easiness that was usually between them replaced by an awkward wariness. He wanted the easiness back. He wanted her to smile and to laugh. He wanted her to like him again.

He didn't know why that was so important to him, but it was. He would make it right between them. He had to.

"Beth?" he murmured.

She turned to him. "Hmmm?"

"I want to show you something."

"What?"

"At my place."

"Your etchings, perhaps?" She lifted her eyebrows. "Old line, Chance."

Her lips curved into the first semblance of a real smile he'd seen in hours. It warmed him more than he liked to admit. "That did sound pretty lame." He laughed. "But sort of, yeah. Trust me, this is on the up-and-up."

"Said the spider to the fly."

"Is that a yes?"

"Yes."

"Good. We're almost there."

Chance hadn't exaggerated and within ten minutes they were pulling into his driveway. Beth stepped out of the car, studying her surroundings. The exterior of his home was what Beth had expected, low-slung contemporary, lots of glass, but as they moved inside, she was surprised. Basing her expectations on his office decor, she'd expected steel and glass, minimal colors and lines, cool elegance.

She would describe this interior as anything but cool, far from elegant. Surprised, Beth moved her gaze around the room. His home was warm, cozy even. He'd filled it with a mishmash of antiques and contemporary and country French furniture, all put together in a way that was disorganized but somehow chic.

Beth followed Chance as he went through the house, flipping on lights, her surprise growing as she did. The art here bore no resemblance to the sophisticated stuff they carried at Art One. This was naive art, funny little pieces made out of tin cans and discarded wood and magazine clippings, pieces glued together with Elmer's and sprinkled with things like glitter.

Charmed, Beth stopped in front of a particularly delightful tempera painting of what looked like a flying pig. She turned and met Chance's eyes. "I didn't expect this."

Chance stuffed his hands into his pockets, feeling suddenly uncertain and exposed. He called himself fourteen kinds of fool. "Do you like it?"

Beth laughed. "How could I not?" She picked up a crudely crafted clay figure and ran her fingers over its rough edges. She met his gaze again. "Why children's art?"

"Because it's honest." He shrugged. "Direct and uncomplicated." He crossed to her and took the figure from her hands. Her warmth lingered on it, and he clasped the piece gently, absorbing her from the porous surface. "Young children don't have the ability to lie about their feelings, and art is a direct outlet for those emotions. Even when the feelings are sad, they make me feel good. Does that make sense?"

She nodded, then moved her gaze around the room before settling it back on him. "This is what you wanted to show me, isn't it?"

"Yes."

"Why?"

He took a deep breath. "I don't know. It seemed the right thing to do at the time."

"And now?"

"And now I don't know." He set the sculpture down, then immediately regretted it. The action left his hands free and itching to touch her. He shoved them into his pockets instead. "I like you, Beth."

"But?"

He frowned. "I want to be honest with you. I want to clear the air between us."

Beth took in the determined, almost grim, set of his expression, and her stomach tightened. She wasn't certain she wanted to hear what he had to say, didn't think honesty was such a hot idea right now. Turning, she crossed to the picture window that looked out over his sloping backyard. He followed her, stopping so close, she could feel his breath against her back.

Chance gazed at her stiff back and rigid shoulders. He lifted a hand to touch her, then dropped it. "I've told you a little about my parents, a little about their disastrous marriage." He laughed without humor. "They were both volatile, passionate people. They loved each other too much, ferociously even. They were jealous and possessive of each other, of their respective careers. Of my affections.

"They finally divorced," he continued. "But they turned the sum total of that jealousy and possessiveness onto me." He paused, giving in to the urge and touching her hair. "I became a pawn in their emotional game. They used me and my love in order to get back at each other."

Hurt for the boy he must have been curled through her. Beth turned to face him. His words made her ache, made her want to hold and stroke him. Lifting a hand to his cheek, she tenderly caressed it. "Poor Chance."

He covered her hand with his own, savoring her touch for a single moment, before setting her away from him. He crossed back to the funny little ceramic figure. For long moments he stared at it. "You know what else I love about children's art? It's a labor of love, but it's not labored over. It's not so damn . . .

precious." He looked over his shoulder at her. "Does that make sense?"

Knowing what she did of his past and his parents, it made a lot of sense. "Yes," she murmured, crossing to him, her dress rustling against her legs as she moved. She stopped before him and met his gaze. "But what I don't understand is, why you're telling me all this."

Panic shot through him. He didn't know. That was the damnable part. He'd made a life out of not sharing his feelings, of not sharing himself. And here he was, sharing everything.

The truth of that scared the hell out of him.

Even as he called himself a fool, he cupped her face in his palms. "Love ruined our lives, Beth. Not hatred or bitterness. Not jealousy." He lowered his voice. "Love."

"I still don't . . . understand."

Chance dragged his thumbs across her cheekbones. "I promised myself I would never let that happen to me. I vowed I would never put a child through that. I'm never going to fall in love, Beth. I'm never going to marry." He dropped his hands and stepped away from her. "I thought you should know that."

Beth stared at him, realization dawning on her. This was some sort of apology for what had happened between them tonight. Some sort of request for absolution. Anger took her breath, hurt and embarrassment her good sense. "Don't be sorry," she said, her voice shaking. "Be anything but sorry."

"I can't help it. I feel I've taken advantage of you. I feel I've led you on."

"Taken advantage of me?" she repeated, heat stinging her cheeks. "Led me on? I'm not a child, Chance.

Not a teenager who got carried away with an older man's glib line."

She took a step closer him, her anger growing, crowding out hurt and embarrassment, making her want nothing more than to prove her point. "I don't want your regrets. I don't want an apology for your passion. I asked for them, I enjoyed them. And I'm certainly not going to apologize for mine."

"That's not what I meant."

"Isn't it? You feel like you've led on poor, plain Beth. You're afraid naive little Beth will get the wrong idea and hound you." She placed her hands on his chest. "Well, I won't hound you. And I won't expect anything from you because we kissed."

"Beth, I—"

"I'm not a child," she said again, cutting him off, her voice vibrating with fury. Shall I prove it?" Taking his hands, she placed them over her breasts. Her nipples hardened with desire, and she wrapped her fingers around his, pressing him closer. "Does that feel like a child to you?"

Chance sucked in a sharp breath, his arousal instant and overpowering. He moved his hands against her, and the hard points of her breasts scraped against his palms.

Beth leaned into his hands, against him. "Why?" she asked again, fighting for breath. "Why can't you be honest with me? What are you afraid of, Chance?"

Her words struck a nerve. Even as he shook his head in denial of that and the panic that coursed through him, he lowered his mouth to hers in a bruising kiss.

Beth's head fell back under its pressure and she grasped his shoulders for support. A moment later he released her, and she stumbled backward a step.

"I'm not afraid," he said tightly. "I am being honest. I don't want to hurt you. I want to be your friend."

The word cannonballed into her, crushing her. It took the anger, the outrage from her. She fought not to let her devastation show, fought to hold on to her tattered pride. She had offered him everything, and he wanted to be her friend. She'd made a total fool out of herself.

"Fine," she said stiffly, stepping away from him. "I won't push myself on you again. Friends. Colleagues. Nothing more."

"Beth." He reached a hand out to her. "Let's talk about this, let's—"

"I think we've talked enough, Chance." She crossed to where she'd dropped her wrap and picked it up. "Take me home."

Two weeks later Beth gazed into her bedroom mirror. Mercifully, the days since Artful Fools had passed swiftly. The business of art was booming, for which Beth was grateful. It left little time at the office for brooding over Chance or for "friendly" conversation between them.

But the nights had passed with agonizing slowness. She couldn't close her eyes without remembering how she had felt in his arms: alive and free and beautiful. Nor could she forget how she had placed his hands on her breasts or the pitying expression in his eyes when he'd told her he wanted to be friends. It still hurt so badly, it took her breath.

Beth pushed away the pain, focusing instead on the reflection she barely recognized. She looked . . . sexy. She looked confident, world-wise . . . Dear Lord, she looked hip.

Awed, Beth skimmed her gaze over her reflection,

taking in the floral leggings, the dangerously dipping neckline of the oversize T-shirt, the bangle bracelets. She fluffed her hair with her fingertips and studied the effect. She'd never thought herself attractive, had never had a reason to. But now—

"You look wonderful," Eva said, clapping her hands together.

"I do, don't I?" For long moments Beth continued to gaze into the mirror, thinking of Chance once more, wondering what he would think of the new her.

She frowned at the woman in the mirror. She hadn't created a new "her," she'd created a whole new person. It didn't feel right . . . she felt like a phony.

But what other choice did she have? In the time since Artful Fools, Chance had asked again and again about meeting Liza. Eva had been like a bull-dog with a juicy bone between its teeth, and finally, despite both skepticism and dismay, Beth had agreed to the charade. So, putting herself in her grandmother's hands, she had begun her transformation into the sexy, reckless, and daring Liza.

The first thing they did was buy clothes, wild, colorful ones: leggings in bold colors, skirts with saucy little kick pleats, off-the-shoulder tops in soft, sexy fabrics, and pencil-slim jeans.

Beth had argued that one outfit would be enough— she planned to introduce Liza to Chance, then send her sister on an extended trip out of the country. Maybe even concoct a sudden marriage to a reclusive prince. But, as usual, Eva had seen the situation differently, and they'd ended up buying everything "just in case."

Next had come her hair. Eva had insisted she lose the "old lady" hairstyles and wear it in a loose tangle of red waves. Beth admitted to being surprised by the results. Her hair, fine and wavy, couldn't have looked better if it had been professionally crimped. New jewelry, shoes, and cosmetics came next; her grandmother's credit cards had reached their limit.

But the most important transformation had been one of attitude. Eva had coached her on being dramatic and impertinent, on how to move, speak, gesture.

Finally, her grandmother had pronounced her ready.

Now here she stood, staring at a person she barely recognized and wishing she could somehow turn the clock back. Beth swung away from the mirror. "This has gone far enough, Eva. I'm going to tell Chance the truth. His parents were artists, he deals with artists everyday, surely he'll understand why I—"

"Lied," Eva supplied.

Lied. The word sounded so dishonest. So guilty. Beth dropped her face into her hands and groaned. "How did this get so messed up? I didn't mean to hurt anybody, I didn't mean to . . . lie. I just couldn't bear for him to know the sketches were mine." Beth glanced back into the mirror. "You really think I can pull this off?"

"I do." Eva handed her a tube of lipstick. "Besides, would you rather lose your job? Would you rather lose Chance?"

Beth shot her grandmother a startled glance. Was she really that transparent? Heat flooded Beth's face, and her grandmother gently patted her cheek. "You won't regret this, Liza. Just trust me."

With a sigh, Beth did, and forty minutes later Beth—as Liza—stepped into Art One. She'd planned this meeting carefully: she'd asked for the afternoon off, the same afternoon Jody always left early, a day that Virginia, the bookkeeper, was on vacation.

That left Chance. Alone. She'd figured pulling this off would be a lot easier if she didn't have to pass everybody's muster.

Beth rubbed her damp palms together. She would pop in, let Chance meet Liza, and leave. She would trump up reasons never to see him again, and that would be that.

Putting a saucy spring in her step, Beth headed for Chance's office. She stopped in the doorway, her heart thudding uncomfortably against the wall of her chest. Chance stood with his back to her, staring out at the spring day. She drank in the sight of him, the soft, dark shirt and slacks, the way the fabric stretched across his broad shoulders, the way it molded other places, places she had no business noticing.

She jerked her gaze back up. Would Liza notice such things? Probably. And dear Lord, the sister she'd created would probably comment.

Sucking in a steadying breath, Beth stepped fully into Chance's office. "Anybody home?" she asked deepening her voice just a little, the way Eva had taught her.

Chance turned. Their eyes met. Surprise registered on his features, followed closely by shock. Her heartbeat, already frenetic, doubled its pace. Her legs trembled so badly that for a moment Beth feared she *would* fall flat on her face. Or faint from lack of oxygen to her brain.

What the hell was she doing?

"Beth?" Chance asked, his voice a croak.

Say yes, she told herself. Back out now, before it's too late. Ignoring all good sense, she sauntered into his office. "That's who I'm looking for. I'm Liza."

Several seconds passed. To Beth it seemed like an

eternity. Fainting became an even greater possibility than a moment ago.

"Liza?" Chance repeated, obviously stunned. He took a step closer. "Beth didn't tell me you . . . and she . . . were twins."

Beth swallowed, the urge to confess all warring with the absolute and paralyzing fear of doing just that. She cocked her head and slanted him a coquettish glance. "Then I have two reasons to be annoyed with her."

"Two?"

"Mmm-hmm." Beth moved her gaze brazenly over him, feeling at once shocked and liberated by her own behavior. "She didn't tell you that she and I were identical twins, and she didn't tell me that you were so . . . yummy."

Chance laughed and shook his head. "I don't think I've ever been called that before."

Beth felt her cheeks heat and cursed the color. "Somehow I doubt that, Mr. Michaels."

"Chance," he corrected, closing the distance between them and holding out his hand. "And believe me, I would have remembered if I had."

Beth took his hand, hoping he wouldn't notice the tremor in hers. He stared down at their joined hands for a moment, then lifted his gaze back to hers. "The likeness is amazing."

The blood rushed to her head, and Beth slipped her hand from his. She turned away from him on the pretense of interest in a piece of art. "My sister said you wanted to meet me," she murmured, picking up the bronze sculpture. She looked over her shoulder at him. "Why?"

"Curiosity."

She set the sculpture down. "Well, now you have."

She flashed him a cocky smile, then started toward the door. "Tell Beth I stopped by."

"Have a drink with me."

Beth stopped, but didn't turn, using the moment to collect herself. When she finally glanced back over her shoulder at him, she hoped he saw a self-confident woman accustomed to turning down drink invitations.

She lifted her lips in a small smile of regret. "No can do, Chance. Thanks anyway."

"Another time, then?"

"I don't think—"

"I'd like to talk to you about your paintings."

"My paintings?" she repeated, suddenly breathless.

"I saw some sketches Beth brought here by mistake. They intrigued me."

Her work intrigued him. He wanted to talk about it.

A dozen different emotions tumbled through her, not the least of which was the desire to say yes. But every moment she prolonged this charade, the more entangled in it she became.

"I'd like that," she said finally, hesitantly. "But I have some things I have to do. . . . Someone I have to . . . meet."

Chance checked his watch. "I have to finish up here, too. Why don't I meet you at the Dana Point Coffeehouse in an hour? Would that give you enough time?"

Feeling as if she were stepping off the edge of a cliff, Beth said it would.

Chance arrived at the coffeehouse early. He chose a table on the sun-sprinkled patio, ordered an espresso, and waited, his thoughts filled with Beth.

But then, since the night of Artful Fools, a moment hadn't passed when his thoughts hadn't been filled with Beth. The memory of their kiss, of their disturbing words later, had lingered, interfering with business, penetrating sleep. He'd wake up thinking of her, wanting her. And aching in a way he never had before.

Frowning, Chance forced his thoughts away from Beth. For a moment, when he'd first seen Liza, he'd been so startled by her resemblance to Beth, he'd almost thought they were one and the same person. But then she'd moved and spoken. Chance smiled at the memory. She'd called him yummy, for Pete's sake.

How could two people—even identical twins—be so much alike yet so different?

His espresso arrived, and he took a sip of the strong, thick brew. Liza's eyes were exactly the color of Beth's, the light, clear blue of a spring sky. And she had the same disarming way of looking at him— directly and without pretense.

Chance stopped on the thought. He hadn't realized how much Beth's eyes affected him. Until now.

He frowned, uncomfortable with that realization. But more uncomfortable with the dawning truth that he'd noticed a lot about Beth. Like the way she caught her bottom lip between her teeth when feeling insecure or vulnerable, or the soft spot she had for hard-luck stories and stray pets. Or the way she made him feel when she smiled at him, big and bold and all man.

Chance shook his head in denial of his thoughts. Liza was the kind of woman who interested him. Brash, worldly, and a bit cynical, sure of herself. With her he would be on even footing.

In a way he wasn't with Beth.

Chance took another sip of the espresso. Even after only one meeting with Liza, he understood her and knew she understood the kind of man he was. Liza wouldn't expect things he couldn't deliver. Her expectations from a man-woman relationship were direct, uncomplicated. He'd dated a dozen women like her; she wasn't a mystery.

Beth was. Soft and gentle and sweet. Vulnerable. Beth made a man think of things he'd promised himself he never would, made a man forget hard-learned lessons about self-preservation. She wasn't for him.

Then why was he sitting here wishing with everything he had that it was Beth meeting him instead of her twin?

Annoyed with his own thoughts, Chance flexed his fingers. He didn't need any mysteries in his life. He didn't need complications. And he was not about to forget the lessons of his childhood.

Artful Fools had been a mistake. Their kiss had been an aberration brought on by the heady scent of her perfume, the moonlit night, his own restlessness.

Chance tapped his index finger against the side of his cup, ignoring the voice inside his head that called him a liar, forcing his thoughts to Liza's art. The first time he'd looked at Liza's sketches, he'd felt a stirring, an excitement he'd felt every other time he'd discovered rich, unplumbed talent. He'd studied those sketches, had thought about the things Beth told him about Liza's artwork. The excitement he'd felt hadn't dimmed over these past weeks. If anything, he'd become almost obsessed with the images.

The time had come to see them.

Chance looked up and saw her. Liza stood in a patch of sunlight, her hair a halo of fire around her head, her expression vulnerable. As he gazed at her, he thought of Beth and of a memory from his childhood—of that moment he'd realized that the mess of his parents' marriage had nothing to do with hate but everything to do with love.

Liza's gaze found his then, and the breath hissed from his lungs. Liza and Beth were the same person.

Ridiculous.

He shook his head to clear it, unnerved by his imaginings. Was he so obsessed with Beth that he couldn't even separate her from her sister?

Liza smiled and crossed to him. "Sorry I'm late."

"You're not." Chance signaled the waiter. "I was just enjoying an espresso and the last of the day."

Grateful for the distraction, Beth studied the purpling sky. "This is my favorite time of day. There's a quiet, a hushed quality to it, as if all of nature is preparing for sleep." She closed her eyes and drew in a deep breath. "I can smell the ocean. It's delicious, don't you think?"

Liza's words were soft, too soft for the woman he had pegged her to be. They reminded him of her sister. Chance stared at her, the sense that something was not right eating at him.

The waiter arrived then, and Chance opened his mouth to ask Liza what she would like, then shut it as she looked over and smiled, first at him, then the waiter.

"A chocolate cappuccino," she told the young man. "Extra whipped cream." As the waiter walked away, she flashed Chance another saucy smile. "I like my sweets."

"So does your sister. Like her sweets, that is. I caught her eating chocolate chips the other morning. She keeps a bag stashed in her file cabinet."

Beth didn't know what to say; she found it disconcerting to have someone commenting about her to her. "We're a lot alike," she said finally.

"But you're also very different."

"Yes." Beth lowered her eyes to her hands, realizing to her horror they were clasped nervously in her lap. She relaxed them. "We are."

"The differences are obvious." Chance rested his elbows on the table and leaned conspiratorially toward her. "In what ways are you alike?"

She looked up at him through what she hoped were provocatively lowered lashes. "I'd rather hear about you."

"Would you?"

"Mmm-hmm." She trailed her fingers back and forth over the lacy wrought-iron tabletop, acknowledging that bantering would be the best way to keep him at bay, but honest enough to admit that hadn't a thing to do with it.

Heaven help her, she was enjoying herself.

Beth swallowed. She couldn't get caught up in this game. She couldn't begin believing her own fantasy. If she did, she would be hurt.

With a sinking sensation, Beth realized she'd been caught up in the game from the moment it had begun. She'd wanted to believe all along.

She flashed him a brilliant smile. "Tell me something about Chance Michaels. Something I wouldn't know from looking at you or reading a bio."

"Let's see . . ." Chance paused. "I like gangster movies and buttered popcorn, even if neither is very good. As a youth, I longed to be a professional tennis player, but I gave up the idea when I discovered girls."

"Girls? And why was that?"

He smiled wickedly. "I didn't have time to practice anymore. Tennis, that is."

"Any regrets?"

"Are you kidding?"

He wiggled his eyebrows, and she laughed. "I guess not."

Her coffee came then, and she pretended great interest in it, adding sugar, stirring and tasting, using the time to collect her thoughts. This was not proceeding according to her plan. She was flirting with him, for heaven's sake. She was trying to attract him.

But she wanted him to be attracted to *her*, not a figment of her imagination. She was in deep, deep trouble.

"Your turn." Chance propped his chin on his fist. "After all, fair's fair."

"All right," she said almost defiantly, wishing she could blame anyone but herself for this messy situation. "I go gaga over all holidays, but especially Christmas. I like rainy mornings and the sound of thunder—neither of which I get too often out here. And I positively adore listening to jazz while eating anchovy pizzas."

He lifted his eyebrows. "Anchovies?"

"Mmm-hmm." She smiled. "But don't offer me an olive, olives are my mortal enemies."

He laughed. "How about drivers who don't use their turn signals."

"Despise them. And their counterparts who refuse to get out of the passing lane even though they have no intention of passing anyone. How about you?" She took a sip of her cappuccino. "Any pet peeves, Mr. Michaels?"

Chance thought for a moment. "Unjustified arrogance and liars."

The coffee lodged in her throat; Beth worked to

swallow it and her panic. "Really?" she managed after a moment.

Chance shrugged and laced his fingers around his cup. "Okay, maybe arrogance isn't so bad. But I won't put up with phonies or deceit."

Beth stared at him, feeling as if the world had just shifted on its axis. A moment before, she had been debating telling him the truth. She couldn't now. Or ever. Eva had been right—if she had come clean, he would have fired her. And when the truth came out—and it would—he would never understand. Or forgive her.

She blinked against the tears that stung the back of her eyes, realizing that he'd asked her a question. "I'm sorry, what?"

"How long have you been painting?"

Her hands trembled and she curled them around her cappuccino cup. "Forever. It's the only school subject I remember enjoying."

Chance leaned back in his chair. "Did you go to art school instead of a university?"

"No." Beth sipped her cooling drink, insecurity barreling over her. "Kansas State. And before you ask, my degree's in business."

"Odd choice."

"Not if you're Suzannah and Burt Waters's child." She met his gaze then. "Why so much interest?"

Chance lifted his eyebrows. "You are aware that I'm an art consultant, and that I find and launch talent."

"Of course. I'm . . . Beth's your assistant."

He shook his head, his expression bemused. "Don't mind me, I'm just used to artists being a little more impressed with that. And a little more excited when I express interest."

"Is that what you're doing? Expressing interest?"

"I thought so." He downed the last of his now-cold espresso, then set the cup carefully on the saucer. "Is that okay? Or should I drop this now—"

"No, of course it's okay. I'm just . . ." She lowered her gaze to her cappuccino, then looked back up at him. "What would you like to know?"

"Are you represented by anyone? A gallery? Another art consultant or representative?"

"No."

"Many juried shows? Invitationals?"

Beth shook her head. "No again."

"May I ask why not?"

"I don't paint for money or acclaim," she said, inching her chin up. "Got a problem with that?"

"Should I?"

Beth flushed and looked away. "I'm sorry. I . . ." She searched for the right words, then decided on the real ones, the ones from her heart. "I'm . . . vulnerable about my work. It means everything to me, and I can't stand the thought of . . . it being . . ." She lifted her hands, palms up. "I don't show it much. At all, really."

Chance reached out as if to touch her, then dropped his hand. "What I've seen is interesting," he said softly. "In fact, more than interesting. But I can't truly evaluate until I've viewed the actual work."

"I see." She heard the hope, the anticipation that trembled in her voice and cursed it. Liza would not be so insecure, Liza would not be so vulnerable. Even about her art.

But she wasn't really Liza. Beth caught her bottom lip between her teeth and gazed helplessly at him.

Chance sucked in a sharp breath. Liza looked exactly like Beth. He frowned. Of course she did. Liza always looked exactly like Beth. That's why they were called identical twins.

Images from the times he and Beth had spent together flashed, kaleidoscope fashion, through his head. Beth . . . passionate and pliant in his arms. Beth . . . her eyes glazed with need, clouded by hurt. Beth . . . vulnerable and uncertain, catching her bottom lip between her teeth.

Liza wasn't shy and soft and heartbreakingly vulnerable. Liza didn't make him feel possessive and protective.

And yet, for that split second, she had been all those things. And so had he.

Stunned, Chance lifted his eyes back to Liza's. What he was thinking was impossible. Preposterous. Why would Beth pretend to be someone she was not? What could she hope to gain by such a thing? But how, he wondered, could two such supposedly different people, even though identical twins, be so much alike?

They couldn't.

Anger rushed through him, even as he told himself he'd lost his mind. The Beth he knew was shy but direct and honest. She would never do something like this. And yet . . . he was certain his instincts weren't wrong.

He had to know. And if she had tried to trick him, he wanted to know why. He had two ways of finding out: ask her or spend a little more time with her and unearth the truth himself. Only one way guaranteed the truth.

Coming to a decision, Chance reached across the table and caught her hand. "I'd like to see you again," he said, trailing his index finger over it, slowly from wrist to thumb.

"To view my paintings?"

"No. I mean, I want to look at your work, but I want to see you again for . . . you."

For a moment Beth's heart stopped beating, then began a wild rapping against the wall of her chest. She wanted to go so badly, but the desire was irrational, irresponsible. Impossible.

She pushed the want away and tossed her head back. "My, my, Mr. Michaels, that's rather forward."

He pressed his finger to the pulse that beat wildly at her wrist, then smiled. "I'm a forward kind of guy."

"I think I'll pass anyway."

"I'll call."

"No again."

"Why not? You want to."

What could she say? That she couldn't because she didn't exist? Or that her twin sister would be brokenhearted if she did? She'd slipped over the edge of reason—she was angry and jealous over Chance's interest in a person who was also her.

"Is . . . Beth the reason you won't go?"

Her breathing stopped. "What could she have to do with this?"

He twined their fingers and leaned toward her, searching her expression. "Exactly my question."

Beth tugged her shaking hand from his grasp. "You're not my type. That's all."

Chance narrowed his eyes. She looked positively panicked; he pushed harder. "I'm exactly your type. And you're mine. We both know it."

"Do we?" She lifted her eyebrows coolly, haughtily. "Excuse me, I think I'll go powder my nose."

Aware of his eyes on her back, she sashayed slowly to the ladies' room even though her every instinct pressed her to gallop. Once inside, she leaned against one of the tile walls, breathing heavily. The tile was cold against her heated skin, and Beth was grateful for the shock.

A woman came out of one of the stalls and looked

oddly at her, and Beth managed a weak smile. Moving to the sink, she splashed cold water on her wrists and neck, then stared into the mirror.

She wanted to see him again. Not at the office. Not as employer and employee or as friends. But as man and woman. Even though it wasn't *her* he wanted, even though it was madness, she wanted to be with him. Beth wet a paper towel and pressed the cold cloth to her flushed cheeks. She had to tell him no, had to end this now. The situation was already too complicated.

But she ached to kiss him.

He'd kissed her as Beth. She squeezed her eyes shut against the memory. But he didn't want mousy little Beth who had never been any good with men, especially at attracting them. Chance wanted the bold and self-confident Liza. Chance desired a figment of her own imagination, the woman she'd always wanted to be but hadn't had the guts to.

It shouldn't hurt. But it did, deeply and to the bone.

Beth stared at her fantasy self in the mirror. What would happen if she went for it? Why not take her fantasy all the way? Chance had proclaimed himself a confirmed bachelor; he ended every relationship before it got serious. He liked to have fun.

She'd never had fun. She'd never allowed herself a real-life fantasy.

She would be hurt. She would lose her job.

Both of those were givens already.

Beth closed her fingers around the damp paper towel, crushing it. If she didn't grab this opportunity, she wouldn't get . . . anything.

She wanted Chance. She wanted to be with him. Even though it was madness, even though she would be hurt.

Beth took her lipstick out of her purse. Marvelous Melon. She applied some of the color, then shook her head. Maybe she really was a multiple personality, but the truth was, she liked being Liza. She felt free, liberated. As Liza, she was able to say anything, whatever she felt, without fear of embarrassing herself. Without the damnable cloak of timidity she always wore.

If she'd decided to live out a fantasy, she might as well do it to the hilt. Have fun with it, pull out all the stops. Beth recapped the lipstick, tossed it into her bag. And that meant acting on her feelings for Chance. That meant being a bold, sensual, and confident woman.

The thought terrified her. It exhilarated her.

Choosing exhilaration, Beth headed back out to the patio.

The sun had begun its final dip in the west, and the sky behind Chance had transformed into brilliant palette that rivaled any she'd ever used. Beth paused a moment and gazed at him, regret arcing through her. If only he wanted *her* . . . Beth. If only . . .

She let her breath out in a determined rush and started across the patio. He didn't. So she might as well stop wishing for the impossible and start living for the attainable.

With a calm and self-confidence that surprised her, Beth slipped back into her chair and flashed Chance a brilliant smile. "Where were we?"

He met her eyes. "We were talking about your sister."

"Funny, I don't remember that."

"No?" Chance caught her hand. Running his finger across her knuckles, he dipped it into the juncture between her thumb and first finger. "Memory can be a selective thing. Just as truth can. What is it you remember?"

Beth worked to even her breathing. "An invitation," she said with a calm she far from felt. "Something about anchovy pizzas and . . . bowling. Tomorrow night." She saw she'd caught him by surprise, and she laughed. "We did a lot of bowling back in Kansas."

"I haven't been since I was a kid."

"Me either." She batted her eyelashes in exaggerated and contrived innocence. "Perhaps a small wager would be fun? The loser buys the pizza?"

"You're pretty good at this, aren't you?"

She arched an eyebrow. "This?"

He paused, then smiled. "Bowling, I mean."

"No." She pouted prettily. "It's been so long, I probably won't even be able to find the pins."

Six

"Lady," Chance said to her a day later, "you are a hustler."

Beth looked at Chance, startled by the serious tone of his voice. "What do you mean?"

Chance held her gaze a moment, then tapped the score sheet. "That's three strikes in a row."

"In bowling, we call that a triple."

"Like I said, you're a hustler."

Laughing, she stood and dusted her fingers with a powder bag. "Just call me Lucky Liza."

"Lefty is more like it." Chance mock-growled. "You're up."

"My, my, Mr. Michaels, a poor loser? I never would have expected it." She crossed to the ball exchange and lifted her bowling ball.

"Not a poor loser, Liza. I don't like losing at all." Chance met her eyes once more. "And I don't like being had."

At that comment, Beth's heart stopped. The day and a half since she'd agreed to this date had been agony . . . and ecstasy. She'd vacillated between calling the date—and this whole crazy stunt—off and being too excited to sleep.

But she hadn't called it off, and she was having a great time even though she pretended to be someone she wasn't, even though she'd slipped into the role so effortlessly, it scared her silly.

Then, every so often, Chance would say something that brought her smack-dab back to reality and reminded her just how absolutely insane this charade was.

Beth slipped her trembling fingers into the ball's finger holes and tossed her head back with a cockiness she far from felt. "Still sounds like sour grapes to me."

Ignoring his muttered comment, she positioned herself on the alley and lined up her shot. Eyes on her mark, she approached, swung and released the ball, then watched it sail down the lane, striking just to the right of the head pin. The pins exploded at the impact, all ten flying back into the pit.

"Yes!" Beth swung around, licked the tip of her index finger and touched it to her hip while making a hissing sound.

Chance leaned back in his chair, disgusted. "Is there any way to cheat at this game?"

"Are you accusing me of cheating?" she asked, sauntering back to where he sat.

"Not at all," he said easily. "Just thinking about trying it myself."

Beth leaned against the scoring table and smiled down at him, her hair tumbling over her shoulder. "I did a lot of bowling in Kansas."

"You said that before."

"Did I?" Beth managed, her heart beating slowly, heavily against the wall of her chest.

"Mmm-hmm." Chance reached up and caught a lock of her hair and wrapped it around his finger. "How about your sister?"

"My sister?"

"I thought you had only one."

"I do." She swallowed. "Just Beth."

He lowered his eyes to her lips, then lifted them back to hers. "So, did . . . 'just Beth' do a lot of bowling too?"

"As a matter of fact, yes. You ready to call it quits?"

"No way." When she made a move to straighten, he tugged gently at her hair, inching her head more toward his. "Are you? Ready to quit, that is."

"Why would I be?" she murmured. "I'm winning."

"So you are." He tugged again, until her mouth hovered a fraction above him. "Remember . . . Liza, the game's not over until it's over." He brought her mouth to his.

Beth shuddered as Chance's lips brushed over hers. She dropped her hands to his shoulders, the raucous sounds of the bowling alley fading until all she heard was the thunder of her heart. And the sound Chance made, deep in his throat, male and satisfied.

Wishing she could deepen the kiss, Beth dug her fingers into her palms until her nails bit into her flesh. She wanted to so desperately, she trembled with the need. But she couldn't. She wasn't Lisa. She was Beth. And she was scared witless.

Chance broke the contact, moving a breath away, his fingers still wound in her hair. Their eyes met. His were smoky with passion, crinkled at the corners with amusement.

"I think I like pushy redheads," he murmured.

It took Beth a moment to recover her poise—and to

get back into character. When she did, she narrowed her eyes. "It seems to me, the redhead isn't the pushy one around here."

"Really?" Chance laughed and let her hair slip through his fingers. "How about a lesson, Red?"

She arched her eyebrows. "Dare I ask, a lesson in what?"

"Bowling. Of course." He arched his eyebrows and stood. "What else could I have meant?"

Her lips still burned from the touch of his, and annoyed, she said boldly, "You tell me."

"I think I'll pass. For now. So, how about that lesson?"

Beth silently cursed his effect on her. "You don't mind getting a lesson from a woman in the middle of a place crowded with men whose first names are Macho and whose main form of sustenance is beer?"

"My ego can take it."

"Why aren't I surprised by that?"

Chance laughed, not at all offended. "Birds of a feather."

She wished. If she had a quarter of Chance Michael's self-confidence, she wouldn't be in this impossible situation. "Okay, then," she said, dusting off her hands on the seat of her pencil-leg jeans and crossing to the ball return. "Like a lot of inexperienced bowlers, you throw a straight ball. That's okay. Men can do pretty well that way, simply because of their strength."

She picked up her ball and cradled it in the crook of her arm while she spoke. "The problem with a straight ball is, you don't get the pin action you do throwing a hook. Consequently, you won't throw as many strikes, and you'll leave a lot of splits."

She slipped her fingers into the ball, demonstrating how he should hold it. "Cup the ball. Like this. Then when you release it, flatten your hand back out. The shifting position of the hand during the follow-through causes the ball to hook into the pocket."

Chance imitated her movements. "Sounds easy enough." He set his ball back in the return and folded his arms across his chest. "How about a demonstration before I try it?"

The tone of his voice was bland, his expression a study in innocence. But his eyes danced with devilry. He looked like a ten-year-old waiting for his teacher to sit on a whoopie cushion. Beth shot him a skeptical glance. "What's the gag?"

He lifted his dark eyebrows, all wounded honor. "I beg your pardon?"

"The gag. The catch. The gotcha."

He held up his hands. "Are you feeling guilty about something? All I want is to see the technique in action before I try it myself."

Her breath caught. His words were harmless enough, nothing in his tone or expression suggested he was suspicious of her, and yet she felt more and more like a cornered mouse.

Maybe it was the pluck of her own conscience, she rationalized. "What would I have to feel guilty about?"

Chance shrugged and folded his arms across his chest once more, his gaze never wavering from hers.

She swore. "All right, I'll demonstrate."

Crossing to the approach, she lined up her shot. Acutely aware of his gaze on her behind, she started, then stopped, then started again.

Shaking her head, she told herself to concentrate. She'd bowled hundreds of games while others looked on; he probably wasn't even looking at her. She peeked over her shoulder at him. He was, indeed, staring at her behind.

"Stop that."

"What?" he asked innocently, lifting his gaze to hers.

"Staring like that. I can't concentrate."

"Really?" When he smiled, there was nothing innocent about the curving of his lips. "But I was only studying your . . . form. Bowling form, of course."

"Of course." Determined not to let him throw her, she started her approach.

"Nice . . . follow-through," Chance murmured as she bent to release the ball, the tone in his voice pure wolf.

The ball flew into the gutter. Beth whirled around, cheeks flaming.

Chance smiled. "Gotcha."

"That was dirty pool."

"Mixing your sport metaphors?" He raised his eyebrows and made a clucking sound with his tongue.

Beth glared at him and straightened her spine. She would not let him affect her game. She simply would not. Retrieving her ball from the return, she approached the markers once more.

This time, as she bent to release the ball, he whistled low and appreciatively. The ball slipped from her fingers and hit the wood lane with a loud— embarrassingly loud—thud. She swung back around, teeth gritted.

He smiled, slow and sexy. "I do *so* like those jeans . . . Liza."

"This isn't very sporting of you."

"On the contrary, I think it's quite sporting."

He threw next. She whistled, cat-called, and murmured her approval, but to no avail. Not only did his concentration not waver, but he threw a perfect right-hander's hook. The ball struck in the pocket, all tens pins tumbled. He turned toward her, his smile impossibly smug.

"Save it, Michaels." She stood and started to brush by him; he stopped her by catching her hand. Looking deeply into her eyes, he brought her hand to his mouth and slowly, lingeringly kissed each one of her fingertips. "Good luck."

Her pulse went wild; her concentration took a permanent leave of absence. She threw two more gutter balls.

Beth whirled back around, fists on hips. "You've found a way to cheat."

"Me?" He pointed to his chest. "Cheat?"

"Yes." She advanced on him slowly, menacingly. "And you'll be sorry. I have my ways."

"I'll just bet you do."

She stopped before him. "You're not taking me seriously, Mr. Michaels. That's a mistake."

"But I am." He moved toward her, not stopping until their bodies brushed. He lowered his voice. "You can't imagine how seriously I'm taking this." She started to move away from him, but he caught her hands so she couldn't. "And you can't imagine how much I want to kiss you."

Chance wasn't lying; he wished he were. He wanted her so much, he ached with it. Even though he was all but certain he was being had. Even though every time she spoke she proved herself more of a liar, he still wanted her.

"Stop it," she whispered, her voice hoarse.

"Why?" He brought her hands to his chest and held them there. He searched her expression, acknowledging that she pulled at him in ways no other woman had ever been able to, acknowledging that if he wasn't careful, he would be caught in his own trap. "Why should I stop?"

"I don't know. I can't . . ." She shook her head and let her words trail off.

He lowered his lips to hers, stopping a fraction before touching them. Her trembling breath whispered against his mouth; his gut tightened. "Can't what?" he pressed. "Talk to me . . . Liza"

And tell him what? she wondered dizzily. That she wanted to be with him, to make love with him. Or that she was a liar?

Beth jerked away from him. He let her go without a fight. "What's going on?" he asked softly. "Is there something you want to tell me?"

"No. And nothing's going on. I'm ready to get out of here, that's all. I'm hungry."

Chance gazed at her for a moment, then smiled. "So am I. Shall we?"

They went to a hole-in-the-wall joint named, appropriately, Just Great Pizzas. What the dimly lit restaurant lacked in decor and service it made up for in taste, but as Chance studied Beth across their table, he wished he'd chosen one of the brightly lit chains.

"Penny for your thoughts," he murmured, watching as she fidgeted with her flatware.

She looked up at him, blushing guiltily. "Never heard of inflation?"

He smiled. "And I thought you were going to be a cheap date."

She attempted a grin and failed. "It really smells great in here."

"You're in for a treat." Leaning across the table, he

caught her fluttering fingers. They were cold and he rubbed them between his. "You're on edge. Is something wrong?"

She held his gaze for a moment, the look in hers soft and sad. "Nothing I can talk about."

He frowned. "You don't trust me."

"It's not that," she said quickly.

"No?"

"No." She shook her head. "I just can't. Not yet anyway. Okay?"

Her eyes pleaded for understanding, and he silently swore. She was feeling vulnerable; now was the time to push. Instead he nodded. "Okay."

Their pizza came then, and they ate in almost total silence. When they'd finished and the waitress had brought the bill, Beth looked at him in question. "Do you still want to see my art?"

"Of course."

"How about now?"

Her voice shook, and Chance drew his eyebrows together. He'd never before dealt with an artist who was so shy about showing her work. In fact, artists usually begged him to take a look at their work. They sought him out. He got the feeling this was the last thing in the world she wanted to do, that, like a dentist appointment, she just wanted to get it over with.

He nodded. "Let's go."

Thirty minutes later Beth unlocked her apartment door. Chance stepped into the apartment, taking in the two beanbag chairs, the single ancient floor lamp and makeshift coffee table. He looked at Liza. "I didn't know you and Beth lived together."

"Yes." She cleared her throat. "We . . . share this apartment."

"I see. Is she home?"

Beth shook her head. "No, she's not."

"You're sure?"

"Yes. She was . . . going out tonight."

"Too bad," he said easily. "I would have liked to say hello."

"Yes, well . . ." Beth took a step backward. "Would you like a glass of wine?"

"Sure."

She hesitated. "I . . . we haven't restocked our kitchen. Would you prefer a paper cup or a coffee mug?"

"Surprise me."

She hesitated a moment longer, then turned and started for the kitchen. When she'd disappeared through its swinging door, Chance wandered around the living room. The walls were bare save for a few family photos, which he glanced at, and a handful of art posters he recognized. And nothing else.

Why hadn't she displayed any of her art?

"I'd forgotten about a couple of tumblers that escaped the thieves. They're big, but at least they're glass."

Chance swung away from a grouping of photos. Beth handed him a tumbler, and he noticed her fingers trembled. He took a sip of the wine, gazing at her over the top of the glass. "You're not pictured," he said after a moment.

"What?" She cupped her hands around her glass.

He took another sip of the wine and motioned to the photographs, watching her closely. "All these family photos, and you're not in one of them."

She looked blankly at him for a moment, then shifted her gaze to the wall and row of framed pictures. "I hate being photographed."

The panic in her eyes pulled at him, and he called himself a fool. Why should he feel sorry for her? Why should he feel guilty? He wasn't the one who was lying. He narrowed his eyes. "Odd, even so. Most parents force their kids to be photographed."

The blood drained from her cheeks, and she turned away from the wall. "My studio's this way. Are you ready to . . . take a look?"

He said he was, and she led him to her studio, opened the door and flipped on the lights. He stopped in he doorway; his breath catching, his mind emptying of everything but the view before him.

Her studio was filled, stuffed even, with her work. Paintings hung on every available inch of wall space, and canvases were stacked against the rest. Bathed in color and energy and light, the room seemed to glow with a life of its own.

His heartbeat heavy and fast, Chance stepped into the room. Her artwork was everything he'd hoped it would be. His instincts had not let him down—Beth had "it," that indefinable something, that magic— the ability to move or excite or stir with nothing more than the stroke of color on canvas.

Chance stepped farther into the room, aware of Beth beside him, her fear an almost palpable thing. He didn't turn to her, didn't speak. His thoughts, his concentration, were for the images before him.

He circled the room, inspecting, studying, taking his time. He flipped through the stacks of canvases. Delicate oranges trailed across the surfaces of the paintings like tails of comets, bold reds zigzagged, pinks glowed, whites decorated with the quality of fine old lace. Her shapes were just as delicate, just as evocative. Soft and round—like a woman or fresh, ripe fruit. Open shapes whose edges rippled, images that called to the heart of sensitivity and vulnerability.

The images touched him. They moved him.

Chance frowned. But where and how to market? These pieces were too gentle to just drop into the current New York scene, with its love of bold, at times even discomfiting, expressionism, too whimsical for L.A., too straightforward for Chicago. Great was always a step beyond fashionable, and because of that, difficult to sell.

His mind whirling with questions and possibilities, he swung toward Beth and scowled. "Do you have slides?"

She nodded. "Yes."

"Are they good quality?"

"I . . . I think so."

"I'll need them," he said brusquely. "Everything that's current—within the last two years or so." When she didn't move, he raised his eyebrows. "Is there a problem?"

"I . . . no . . ." Beth swallowed and folded her arms around herself. "Say something about them," she whispered. "Anything."

Chance saw then how she shook, how ashen her face, how large her eyes.

"Don't take the slides," she continued, "just because . . . you know. It's not necessary. I'll understand if—"

Chance closed the distance between them and cupped her face in his palms. "I think your work is wonderful."

"Are you sure?"

He smiled. "Yes."

"But you didn't say anything." She searched his

expression. "You looked and sounded so . . . angry. So impatient."

Chance smiled, feeling like both Grinch and Santa Claus. "When confronted with art that excites me, I get lost in it. I forget about being sensitive or thoughtful. I become a bit of a brute. It's the way I am."

"What exactly are you saying?"

He laughed and brushed his thumbs across his bottom lip. It trembled under his caress, and his pulse stirred. "That I think your paintings are special. I don't know if anyone else will. My instincts are usually on the money, but there's always a chance they won't be. And I'm not sure how to market your work. It's different."

Beth smiled, softly and with wonder. She tipped her head back, her breath coming fast, her heart beating faster. "It doesn't matter. You like them, that's enough."

He moved his fingers over her face, exploring, savoring. He smiled. "That makes no sense."

"It does. To me." She wound her arms around his neck and laughed, feeling free and bold and self-confident. "Kiss me, Chance. Kiss me hard."

He did.

Not bothering with preliminaries, Chance settled his mouth on hers with an almost bruising force. Parting her lips, he twined his tongue with hers, exploring the secrets of her mouth.

Just as it had the last time, his arousal, instantaneous and overwhelming, clawed at him. Kissing her wasn't enough. He wanted her closer and deeper. He wanted to bury himself inside her.

Beth whimpered and tightened her fingers in his hair, returning the pressure of his kiss, reveling in him, in the moment, and in the way he made her feel—alive and aching and totally female.

He liked her art, she thought dizzily. He thought it wonderful. Wholly her, her art had nothing to do with Liza, with the character she'd created, with pretense. She had spilled everything she was into and onto those canvases—her heart and soul, her guts.

Just as she spilled all she was into their kiss.

Feeling liberated, she pressed herself against him, telling him without words how she felt and what she wanted. For the first time in her life she felt free to express her needs—to be a woman with strengths and fears, to respond.

Chance muttered something low and fervent against her mouth and backed her up to her worktable. She wound her fingers in his hair. Ironic that in pretending to be someone else, she had found a piece of herself.

Lifting her, Chance sat her on the table. He buried his face against the skin of her neck, breathing in her soft, female scent. A scent at once sweet and secretive and strong. It went straight to his head until all of his senses were filled with her. At that moment he couldn't imagine a time when he hadn't touched her.

Moving aside the neck of her blouse, he trailed his mouth over the curve of her shoulder, the delicate ridge of her collarbone, then lower. Her skin was silky smooth and as white as milk.

Save for the freckles—they dotted her flesh like a sprinkling of brown sugar. Smiling, he kissed each, thinking them small but perfect miracles.

Chance cupped her breasts, then pressed his mouth to the swell of flesh he exposed. The skin there was softer still, whiter, more fragrant. Her nipples hardened against his palms, begging for attention. He lowered his mouth, tasting her through the thin fabric of her blouse and bra. She arched her back and moaned as he did, pressing herself to him as if she couldn't get close enough.

Chance's control, already at the snapping point, slipped more; desire trembled through him until he thought he had to have her or die. The images from her paintings, their spirit, their heart, filled his head. At that moment nothing mattered but the moment and their passion.

Being with her felt right. Touching and kissing her felt righter yet. He wanted to make love with her— more than anything he'd ever wanted and with an urgency that took his breath.

He'd felt this way only once before.

"Beth . . . Beth . . ."

Her name slipped from his lips without plan or pretense. Chance stiffened, realizing with a shock what he'd done. He lifted his head. As he broke their kiss, she opened her eyes and gazed at him, her eyes glazed with passion. She hadn't caught that he'd called her her twin sister's name. No woman—or man—would miss such an unforgivable slip.

He had his proof.

Shaking with an anger that knew no bounds, Chance pulled away from her. Why did knowing for certain make such a difference in the way he felt? Had he been wanting to believe in her innocence all along? "I've got to go," he said, his voice taut with controlled fury.

"Go?" she repeated, not quite comprehending, still dizzy with desire. She fingered the soft weave of his pullover.

"Yes." He moved away from her, forcing her to drop

her hands. The look in her eyes would have torn at him if he didn't know what a consummate actress she was.

What kind of a fool did she take him for? A big one, he acknowledged.

Beth slid off the table, self-consciously straightening her blouse, a dozen different emotions barreling over her, not the least of which was embarrassment. She looked at him, fighting back tears. What had she done? What happened to change him from a heated lover to a cold and angry stranger?

"Do you . . ." She cleared her throat. "Do you still want . . . my slides?"

Chance stopped at the doorway and swung around, pinning her with his angry gaze. "Your slides?"

Confused, Beth clasped her trembling fingers together. "Yes, you said—"

"I know what I said. Bring them to work. I mean," he corrected harshly, "have *Beth* bring them."

She took a step backward, stunned. Chance knew the truth. He knew she'd deceived him. The realization dizzied her, and she pressed a hand to her stomach as if she'd received a blow. What had tipped him off? she wondered, her world crashing around her ears.

He would never understand. Never.

But she had to try to explain. She couldn't let him leave thinking her a . . .

What? A liar?

Beth's eyes filled with tears, and, mustering all her self-control, she held them back. She hadn't meant to hurt him, only to protect herself. Fear didn't excuse her, but surely he could understand the why.

She raced after him, catching him as he opened the door. "Chance, wait! Please—" He whirled around to face her, and her breath caught at the fury in his eyes. "Please, let me try to . . . explain. Let me—"

Muttering an oath, Chance yanked her against his chest and caught her mouth in a bruising kiss. A second later he let her go and she stumbled backward, her eyes wide with shock.

"Don't say anything . . . Liza. Not one more word."

Her tears spilling over, she watched him let himself out.

Seven

Chance stood at his office picture window, gazing out at the new day and thinking of Beth. And of the way she'd tried to dupe him. He'd thought her a woman without wiles, a woman who didn't play games. Everything he'd thought she was had been a lie.

How she must have laughed at him.

He reached out and touched the plate glass with his fingertips, denying hurt, denying that the ache that twisted inside him was pain. Anger, he told himself, balling his fingers into a fist on the hard, unyielding surface. Helpless fury.

He'd spent a sleepless night wondering why she'd done it. The sun had been easing over the horizon when he'd figured it out.

Her art.

Beth had used him to promote her art. It was as simple as that. He'd had artists follow him, camp out on his doorstep, and send gifts; one had even tried to seduce him. But Beth had stooped to a new and elaborate low.

She'd missed her creative calling. She should have been an actress. Like her grandmother.

Anger tightened in Chance's chest, and he swung away from the window and the light that stung his tired eyes. If only he didn't remember the way she'd felt in his arms, if only he couldn't recall the way she'd reacted to his kiss, his caress. Chance scowled. No doubt that had been a part of her act as well.

But the way he'd responded hadn't been part of an act.

And maybe that was the hardest to live with of all.

Chance shook his head against that thought and the others that crowded his mind. Thoughts of his parents, of their hell of a marriage, of their emotional blackmail, their manipulation of his feelings. With the thoughts came a feeling of suffocation, of being torn in two. He hadn't felt those in a long time. He'd promised himself he never would again.

Beth had manipulated him, just as his parents had. Chance swung defiantly back toward the window and the light that spilled through. At least his parents' motivation had been understandable. At least their deceit had had a basis in honest emotions. But this . . .

Chance hardened his jaw. During the dark, sleepless hours, he had decided Beth's deceit was a blessing in disguise. It had reminded him of his vow to never become emotionally entangled with a woman, his promise that he would never put himself in the position of having his emotions manipulated again.

He'd broken his own vow; he had become involved with Beth. He'd been drawn to her vulnerability, her softness. He had begun to care for her.

Chance swore, the ache tightening in his chest, stealing his breath. That woman didn't exist, he reminded himself harshly. Beth Waters was as vulnerable as a barracuda, as honest as the worst politician.

Chance turned his gaze to the painting across from his desk and the bold slash of crimson that trailed across it. Red, he thought. The pet name fit the Beth Waters he had thought he'd known, the one he had begun to fall in love with.

Love? Chance flexed his fingers, denying the truth with everything he had, fighting the urge that raced over him to do violence. How could he have been so blind? So stupid?

Beth's wily grandmother had helped her concoct this scheme, no doubt about it. Well, he'd come up with his own scheme. Confronting and firing Beth would be too humane. Chance smiled grimly and moved to his desk, sliding into the chair behind it. Even though he had his answers, he would continue to pretend he didn't know what she'd done, and he would romance both "sisters." In the process, he would trap her into admitting the truth.

The only part of the equation that perplexed him was what to do about her art. If he didn't promote it, someone else would. He had no uncertainty about that. Beth was a great talent, and there was a monumental amount of money to be made from that talent.

And money hadn't a thing to do with it.

Chance frowned. He couldn't forget her paintings. Their images had stayed with him; even when he'd been fuming over the fool she'd made of him, they'd been on his mind.

His frown deepened. How could she have done it? He picked up a marker and twisted it between his fingers. It was inconceivable to him that the person who had created art with such depth and spirit and sensitivity could so cold-bloodedly lie and manipulate.

But then he'd learned long ago that creative genius and nice didn't necessarily go hand-in-hand.

Chance tossed the marker down. When Beth realized he knew what she'd done, he wanted her contracted to him. Not that he would try to stall her career or hurt her professionally—but she would be uncomfortable, she would always wonder.

He wanted to make her sweat.

Chance smiled. The thought of that was appealing. Very appealing.

Beth stood outside Chance's office door, their weekly agenda clasped in her trembling hands. She took a deep breath, readying herself for what would surely be the most traumatic moment of her life.

She knew what to expect. If Chance's behavior of the night before was any indication, she would be fired. But that wasn't the worst of it, not by a long shot. The worst was knowing Chance would have nothing but disdain for her, and knowing that after this meeting she would never see him again.

Beth squeezed her eyes shut, remembering the way she'd felt in his arms, the freedom, the abandon. Knowing she would never feel that away again hurt so much, it frightened her.

Beth opened her eyes and looked at his door. She couldn't avoid this, couldn't pretend her way out of it. The time had come to face the consequences of her actions.

She peeked in his partially open door, tapping on the doorjamb. He looked up and their eyes met. Regret curled through her, as did love. This was it.

"Chance?" she murmured, her voice thick with emotion. "Could I . . . speak with you?"

For a moment she thought she saw fury in his

expression, and she braced herself. A moment later he smiled and beckoned her into his office. "Good morning."

Confused, Beth stared at him. She had expected anger, disdain, rejection. She had wondered if he would curse her or simply and coldly ask her to clean out her desk. She hadn't prepared for "good morning." She hadn't prepared for warmth.

His smile deepened. "Beth, is something wrong?"

She shook her head, opening her mouth to speak and finding she couldn't. She hesitated a moment longer, then stepped the rest of the way into the room and crossed to the chair opposite his desk. She sank into it, the agenda still clasped in her hands.

"Did you have a good weekend?" he asked softly, looking her straight in the eyes.

Beth shifted in her seat, uncomfortable with the directness of his gaze, totally unbalanced. "It was fine," she said cautiously. "Quiet."

"But you did go out?" Chance picked up a red marker and twisted it in his fingers.

Beth watched him toy with the pen. He wasn't a man who fidgeted. She lifted her gaze back to his and found that he was studying her. Unsettled, she shifted in her seat. "Why do you ask?"

Chance tossed the marker down and leaned back in his chair. He cocked his head and smiled. "I was over at your apartment last night. Visiting Liza. Didn't she tell you?"

If he didn't know, then what had happened last night? She cleared her throat, the memory of what had occurred between them filling her head. "Yes. You came to see her art."

Chance stood and rounded the desk, stopping beside Beth's chair, forcing her to tip her head back to meet his eyes. "Did she tell you what I thought of it?"

"Yes," she murmured again. He hadn't realized the truth—but she would come clean anyway.

She opened her mouth to do just that, then closed it again, calling herself a coward. She couldn't do it. The truth was, she was only ready to face the consequences if she had to. She wasn't ready to say good-bye to Chance.

"Did you bring Liza's slides?" Chance asked.

"Her slides?" Beth repeated, struggling to sound normal but sounding breathless anyway.

"Mmm-hmm." Chance leaned down and tucked a strand of her hair behind her ear. As he did, his fingers brushed her cheek. She shuddered at the sensation. "Don't worry about it, Red. I'll get them from her myself."

That was the name he'd called Liza. She opened her mouth to remind him, then shut it again as she remembered he called her that, too. "Fine. Whatever."

Chance lifted his eyebrows in question. "Do you have a problem with that?"

Of course she did. She didn't want him to see Liza; she didn't want him to refer to her and another by the same name. But how could she tell him she was jealous of her imaginary sister?

"No . . . I . . . of course not." Beth cursed both her telltale blush and her stammering. "We've got a lot on the schedule this week." Beth held the week's agenda out to him. "We're still far from caught up."

Chance reached for the book, but instead of taking it, he caught her hand. He held it in his, running his fingers over hers. "Your hands are just like your sister's."

"We're twins," she said quickly, tugging against

his grasp. He tightened his grip and turned her hand over.

"Of course you are. But still . . ." He traced the lines on her palm. "Did you know that this is the line of creativity?"

"No, I—"

"Yours is long. Like Liza's."

The blood rushed to her head. "Is it?"

"Yes."

He moved his finger hypnotically over the crease in her palm. Her hand trembled; Beth knew he felt it. He'd had to, but he didn't comment.

"Are you creative, Beth?"

He looked deeply into her eyes, and the trembling spread to every part of her. Not trusting herself to speak, she nodded.

He moved on. "And here is your love line. I wonder what this means?" He rubbed his finger against a small break in the line. "Not a broken heart, I hope?"

Without waiting for a reply, he moved his fingers until they circled her wrist. She wondered if he could feel the wild staccato beat of her heart. "Have you ever been wounded by love, Beth?"

He meant to kiss her.

She wanted him to, wanted so badly, she ached. Her breathing light and fast, Beth tipped her head back a fraction more, her lips parting, her eyelids fluttering shut.

He dropped her hand. "I'm moving the Summer Show up a week. Can you be ready to leave for San Francisco day after tomorrow?"

Beth snapped her eyes back open, stunned and embarrassed by her own behavior.

He hadn't meant to kiss her. And even if he had, they couldn't kiss. Or anything else. He was dating . . . her imaginary identical twin sister.

Her life was as baroque as a daytime drama.

If only she was a viewer instead of a participant.

"We'll only be gone overnight," he continued, not looking at her, flipping through their agenda.

Beth stood. "Fine. I'll be ready to go." When he still didn't glance up, she cleared her throat. "Have you picked the artist for the show?"

His fingers stilled on the book, and he lifted his gaze to hers. "Why?"

She jammed her hands into her blazer's pockets, uncomfortable with the look in his eyes. "I'm your assistant. This is the biggest event of our year. The press has been hounding me, and the new artists are whipped into a frenzy. They all just . . . want it so bad. They know that the artist represented in the Summer Show always goes on to become a star."

"And you understand that want, don't you, Beth?"

She understood it, even though she didn't share it for herself. She had never wanted to be a star; she had only ever wanted to create. "Yes," she said softly. "I guess I do."

"I see." Chance closed the agenda and tossed it on his desk top. "And that's the only reason you want to know?"

"Yes. What other reason could there be? I'm your assistant, and I don't understand why you won't share this me."

"Don't you?"

"No, I don't." Suddenly angry, she put her fists on her hips. She was tired of playing this damnable game of cat and mouse. "Is this arrangement working out, Chance? Are you dissatisfied with my performance?"

"Your performance? Your performance has been spectacular."

Beth stared at him, confused. She had the feeling

they were talking about two different things. "If there's something you'd like to say to me, I'd appreciate—"

"You'll understand, Red. Believe me, you will." Chance reached out as if to touch her, then dropped his hand. "I want to keep this to myself a little longer." He flashed her a brilliant smile. "Okay?"

She let out a deep breath. "Okay." She started for the door, then stopped and looked back at him. She found him gazing at her with an almost intense expression on his face. She shuddered, at once warmed and chilled by the look. "Is there anything else?"

Chance blinked. "Yeah, there is. You're the best assistant I've ever had."

Beth let herself out, the strangest sensation in the pit of her stomach. If that were true, why had his eyes been filled with regret?

The next morning Beth dragged herself out of bed and, yawning, pulled on the psychedelic floral print robe that had been a gift from her grandmother the Christmas before. She padded out to the kitchen to make coffee, her thoughts filled with Chance.

After grinding the beans, she filled the kettle with water. While she waited for the water to boil, she stared sightlessly out the window above her sink. The day before had turned out to be an emotional roller coaster, Chance's behavior seesawing between businesslike and outrageously flirtatious. And she had seesawed between believing that he knew she and Liza were one and the same person and believing he didn't know.

Beth frowned. But if he knew, why was he keeping the knowledge a secret from her? Chance had never seemed the type to play games. What could he hope to gain by subterfuge?

The kettle whistled and she poured the boiling water into the filter. Several times the day before, she'd glanced up to find him watching her, the expression in his eyes almost . . . hungry. Beth shuddered, remembering the way her body had responded to that look, with a wild, uncontrollable heat. A heat that had unnerved and excited her.

Timid little virgins weren't accustomed to wanting so desperately, they felt aflame. They weren't accustomed to wanting their bosses to kiss them senseless.

Beth shook her head. Now she was imagining Chance looking at her with hunger in his eyes. Chance wanted Liza, not her.

But she *was* Liza.

Only he didn't know that.

Or did he?

Beth dropped her head into her hands and groaned. Even she was confused. Sometimes she felt like Liza and other times Beth. Sometimes she felt like a combination of the two.

The knock on her front door didn't come as a surprise. Ever since the robbery, Mrs. Beaver had gotten into the habit of checking on all the neighbors first thing in the morning. What the older woman hoped to accomplish, Beth hadn't figured out. But the visits made the lonely woman happy, so Beth humored her.

Leaving her coffee, Beth went to the door. She swung it open in mid-yawn.

"Liza. I see I got you up."

"Chance?" Beth rubbed her eyes.

"The one and only." He trailed his eyes slowly over

her, then brought his gaze back to her face. He smiled wickedly. "Interesting robe."

Beth looked down at herself. Even though her garment was completely concealing, she felt exposed. Beth tightened the robe's sash. "What bring's you out so early?"

"I couldn't reach you yesterday or last night, so here I am."

Which didn't tell her a thing. She frowned and propped one bare foot on top of the other. "Oh."

"Can I come in?" He held up the bag bearing the logo of the Dana Pointe Coffeehouse. "I brought cappuccinos. Sweet, just like you like them."

Beth caught her bottom lip between her teeth. If only he didn't look so irresistible. If only she wasn't in love with him. If only she were dressed.

"I promise to be good."

He flashed her another of his breath-stealing smiles, and she stepped aside. "Okay, come on in. I might have a sweet role or a Danish to go with the cappuccinos."

"Sounds good." He followed her to the kitchen. "You have chairs?"

"And a table." They reached the kitchen, and she motioned to the butcher-block table and four ladderback chairs at its center. "They were delivered yesterday. Have a seat."

He did and she busied herself getting the pastries, plates, and napkins, unable to ignore the way he filled her kitchen, unable to deny how right he looked sprawled in one of her chairs. Beth sighed. Only a fool continued to wish for the impossible.

Chance heard her sigh and tipped his head, studying her while she moved around the tiny kitchen. Her movements were clean, efficient. In the kitchen as she was at the office, Beth was thorough and unflappable; she never rushed. Yet she always got the job done.

But those qualities weren't the reason he couldn't take his eyes off her.

Chance let his gaze rove slowly over her, from her deliciously sleep-tangled hair, to the curve of her hips, outlined by the gentle cling of her robe, to her coral-tipped toes, peeking out from beneath the gown's hem.

Something stirred deep inside him, and he frowned. He'd come this morning as the next step in his plan to trap her. He'd come to collect her slides and give her an agency contract. Not to become more involved with her, not to make love. He had best remember that.

Chance's frown deepened. He suspected Liza was preparing to take the proverbial hike, leaving her sister Beth to take care of any necessary art arrangements with him. As a next move on Beth's part, it made perfect sense.

He had to stop her.

Beth set the plate of Danish on the table, then slid into the chair opposite him. Only then did she meet his eyes. The expression in hers—at once vulnerable and shy and eager—tore at him, and Chance reminded himself what an expert actress she was.

He helped himself to one of the sweet rolls. "Beth said you went to the movies last night."

"Umm, yes." Beth silently cursed the lie. The night before, she had felt so guilty after having talked to him, she had gone to a movie just to keep from having lied again.

His fingers stilled. "Was it any good?"

She really couldn't tell him. She had been so preoccupied with Chance and the triangle she'd created when she'd invented Liza, she'd been unable to concentrate on the film.

She lifted her shoulders. "It was one of those lightweight comedies. It didn't hold my interest."

"Too bad."

She shrugged again. "I went to the dollar cinema. My investment was small."

Silence fell between them. Beth lowered her eyes to her hands, acutely aware of the thinness of her robe and gown, of the intimacy of their surroundings. And of the fact she could refuse him nothing.

The memory of being in his arms, his mouth on hers, flooded her mind. Her nipples hardened; her breath caught. She silently offered him the plate of sweet rolls, working not to meet his eyes, knowing that if she did, he would see the desire that smoldered in hers. "Have another."

"No. Thanks." He pushed his plate aside. "Red?"

Beth met his eyes, then looked away. She would end this charade now. She had to. She couldn't lie any more, couldn't pretend. Better to cut her losses than to bear the agony of helplessly loving him.

Beth dropped her hands to her lap. "I'm glad you're here," she began softly, horrified by the quaver in her voice. She took a deep breath, steadying herself. "I have something I must . . . tell you. This is difficult for me, I know you'll be angry . . . furious even, and I—"

"Don't say any more." Chance stood and rounded the table to where she sat. Squatting down in front of her chair, he covered her hands with his, forcing her to meet his gaze. "I know what you're about to say."

Her hands trembled and she cursed the telltale weakness. "You do?"

"Yes." He wrapped his fingers around hers, surprised by the urgency that coursed through him.

"I'm here this morning because I want to explain my behavior of the other night. I want to apologize."

"That's not it," Beth said quickly. "Please, let me say what I must, and then if you're still—"

"Shh." He placed a finger gently against her lips. They were warm against his skin and trembled slightly. The urge to take them with his own raced over him, and it took everything he had to deny the urge. "Don't say that you don't want to see me anymore, Liza. Say anything but that."

Beth's heart stopped. How could this be happening? How could the thing she desired most be so close yet so far? She lowered her eyes, not wanting him to see the anguish in hers. "Chance, you don't understand."

"You're angry with me." Chance stood and drew her slowly to her feet. He slid his hands from her elbows to her shoulders, then eased her against his chest. "I behaved badly the other night. I'm sorry. Let me try to explain." He pressed his mouth to her hair. "Please, Red. Just listen."

Wanting curled through her. Beth squeezed her eyes shut and flattened her hands against his chest, meaning to push him away. But then she felt the rhythmic pounding of his heart.

Even as she told herself it was wrong, she looked up at him. "What happened the other night?" she asked, the words trembling on her tongue. "Why were you so angry? Why did you run out like that?"

He searched her expression for subterfuge, for calculation. He found hurt and yearning instead. The combination tugged at him. "I got scared," he said simply.

She lifted her eyebrows in surprise. And disbelief. "Scared? You? Of what?"

Chance tangled his fingers in her hair, glorying in

the silky feel of the strands. He smiled. "Of you, Red. Only of you."

Beth shook her head. "Why would I . . . scare you?"

Chance eased her against his chest, all thoughts of revenge gone. At that moment nothing mattered but that she be in his arms. And that she believe him. "I realized I'd begun to care for you. Care in a way I promised myself I never would."

Aching, Beth whispered, "What are you saying?"

"Spend the day with me." Smiling with an easiness he didn't feel, he slipped his arms around her. "Give me another chance."

Beth blinked, surprised by the invitation, more surprised by his mood shift. "Today is a workday."

"Who cares? Let's go to the zoo. Or Disneyland."

"I don't think that's a good idea."

"Is Beth here?" he asked.

"No . . . yes. I mean, she's asleep. I was supposed to wake her up this morning. She's going to kill me."

He tightened his arms. "I'll protect you."

"No, really. You have to leave." She pushed against him.

Chance let her go and checked his watch. "You better get her up, because I need her to get to work on time." He took a step toward her. "Because I'd like to be very . . ." He took another step. "Very . . ." He pulled her back into his arms. "Late."

Beth sucked in a desperate breath. "But Art One . . ."

"Beth can handle it. Get her up and tell her you're going with me."

"No! I mean," she corrected, "I can't spend the day with you." She pushed her hair away from her face. "I have plans."

He caught her hands and pressed his pelvis against hers. "Can any plans be more important than us."

"Us?" she squeaked.

"Mmm-hmm." He bent his head and nibbled at her lips. "You taste like chocolate cappuccino."

She whimpered, her eyes fluttering shut. He moved his fingers in slow circles against her spine. She melted against him.

"Aw, come on," he whispered in her ear. "Let's go out and play today."

Yes jumped to her lips; horrified, she swallowed it. Was she both fool and idiot? Beth shook her head and, stealing herself against the sensations rocketing through her, ducked out of his arms.

Guilt eating at her, she swung away from him. "You know, I think Beth said something about a doctor's appointment today."

"Is she ill?"

"No. One of those routine things. And I really have to do some . . . things."

"Tonight, then?"

"Tonight?" she repeated, peeking over her shoulder at him.

"Mmm-hmm. Maybe Beth would like to join us. It'd be loads of fun."

"Can't." She shook her head, relief flooding over her as she remembered that she really did have plans. "It's Eva's birthday, I . . . we're taking her to dinner."

Chance narrowed his eyes. "I see."

"It's not like that," Beth said quickly. "I want to see you again, it's just that . . ."

"It's just what?" Chance asked quietly, flexing his fingers. "Talk to me . . . Liza."

Beth met his eyes, then looked away. "Things are not as they . . . it's complicated. I . . ."

She let her words trail off, tears springing to her eyes. She wanted to tell him, she did. But she couldn't bear the thought of losing him. *Lose him? Everything they had was based on a lie.*

She wrapped her arms around herself. "I've got my slides ready. If you still . . . want them."

Chance stared at her for a moment, then nodded. "I'll take them with me."

"Okay." Beth hesitated, then started for her studio. "I'll be right back."

Chance watched her hurry from the room, his chest tight with anger. But worse, with disillusionment. For a moment, when he'd seen how distressed she was becoming, he had felt like a heel. For a moment, he had believed the things she said with her eyes. He'd thought himself no better than she.

Then he'd reminded himself what a fool she was making of him. And why.

He moved to the window above her sink and stared out at the California landscape—the once-virgin hills layered with row after row of identical two-hundred-thousand-dollar homes, the perfect Easter egg–blue sky, the lush vegetation kept alive by expensive watering systems.

He'd been right—about her next move, about what she was capable of, about what she wanted.

His victory was a hollow one.

Frowning, he picked up his jacket and shrugged into it. He'd been wrong. He had thought he would enjoy cornering her. He hadn't. He had thought playing her game would satisfy. But it didn't.

He abhorred frauds. And deceit. Yet here he was. But he wasn't about to back out now. He would see this thing through.

San Francisco, he thought, as she reappeared carrying the binder of slides. Before they got on the plane to fly back home, the truth would be out. He would push as hard as he had to, and if that didn't work, he would confront her. He wanted this thing over with.

She smiled tentatively and handed him the package. "Here they are."

He held the sleeves, one after another, up to the light for a quick inspection. "They're very good," he said and slipped them back into their binder. "I'll need you to sign an agency contract. Basically, it grants me sole representation in California and any other region where there's an Art One gallery."

Chance took an envelope from his jacket pocket. "I suggest you have an attorney look it over. It is binding. I'd like it back as soon as possible, as I won't begin marketing your work until I do."

Beth took the contract from him, her hands trembling. "I'll do that."

"It's a big step, Red. I hope you're happy." Without waiting for her to respond, he started for the door. "You better go get your . . . sister up. She's going to be late for work."

Eight

San Francisco. Home of fine chocolates and trolley cars and Fisherman's Wharf. A city defined by old and new, by tradition and trend, and by an exciting mix of cultures. All blended together to create a city rich in flavor and texture, a romantic city. A place for lovers.

Beth craned her neck to see out the taxicab window, then the moment the vehicle pulled to a stop in front of their hotel, she hopped out. Too excited to wait for Chance to pay the driver, she rushed to the corner to watch a trolley car climb the hill that started at the base of their hotel. The driver clanged his bell, and Beth laughed. It was just as she had always imagined it would be.

Chance came up behind her. "This is your first visit to San Francisco."

It wasn't a question, and she grinned up at him. "How could you tell?"

The wind had tugged some strands of her hair free of her braid. Grinning, he tucked them behind her ear. "Oh, I couldn't. You're every inch the bored and cynical world traveler."

She laughed again. "San Francisco was one of the places I always dreamed about visiting. Remember that rice commercial?"

Chance thought for a moment, then hummed the jingle.

"That's it. Every time I'd see that commercial, I'd fantasize about hills and flowers and trolley cars." And romance, she thought. A wild romance with an ardent suitor. She sighed. Some fantasies were too ridiculous to even voice. "Do we need to go right to the gallery?"

"Tomorrow morning. Today and tonight are for us."

Us, she thought. How delicious that sounded— even though he'd said almost the exact thing to Liza only two days before.

Beth stiffened her spine against the thought and the pain that sliced through her with it. For today and tomorrow, she would put Liza and the future out of her mind. She would give herself the gift of these couple of days.

When they returned to L.A., she would tell him. To hell with the consequences. To hell with timidity and fears. The time had come to face the truth.

Beth looked up at him. But for now she would allow herself the pleasure of his company . . . and the illusion of his affections. "What next, then?"

He trailed his thumb across her flushed cheek, then shook his head and dropped his hand. "We should check in."

Beth sighed dramatically. "Must we?"

"We could leave our bags on the street."

"And hope no one picks them up." Beth glanced around. "Everybody looks honest to me."

"Right." Chance laughed and caught her hand. "Come on. We'll just let the front desk know we're here and have our bags sent up. We'll be back on the street in five minutes. I promise."

True to that promise, five minutes later they stood outside their hotel, the city and its endless possibilities sprawled out before them.

"Where do you want to begin?" Chance asked.

"Chinatown," she said without hesitation. "Then chocolates. Then the Wharf, then Russian Hill, then—"

"That's a tall order, lady." Chance grabbed her hand and pulled her toward the trolley stand. "We'd better get going."

They took the trolley to Chinatown and wandered in and out of shops that dealt exclusively in Chinese imports, much of it stuff for tourists. They passed storefronts hung with whole chickens and bottled concoctions and signs done completely in Chinese characters.

Chance laughed and teased and flirted. He seemed content to let her shop, good-naturedly razzing her every time she bought another junky trinket. Occasionally he would touch her cheek or hair, and as they moved along the sidewalks he kept a hand at the small of her back.

His touch both warmed and excited her; she loved him so much she thought she might burst with it. And she felt as though they were lovers. The shopkeepers thought they were—Beth could tell by their glances, their knowing smiles. One even offered Chance a charm that would keep Beth bound to him forever.

He didn't need the charm, Beth thought as, laughing, he bought it. She was bound to him already, in every way and forever.

After a couple of hours exploring Chinatown, they went to Ghirardelli Square, then Fisherman's Wharf. Beth hadn't seen Chance so relaxed since . . . Her eyebrows drew together as she thought. Since before Liza, she realized. She wasn't certain what that meant, and she didn't care. For the moment, he belonged to her. Worries would wait, as would doubts.

As they arrived back at their hotel the sun made its final dip behind the horizon. Chance unlocked Beth's room for her, then swung the door open. She didn't make a move to go inside. Instead, she turned to him and said, "I don't think I've ever had so much fun. Thanks."

Chance wanted to kiss her so badly, the need clawed at him. "I had fun too."

"I wish . . ." She caught her bottom lip between her teeth and shook her head. "Never mind."

He gave in to the need and cupped her face in his palm. She tipped her face into the caress, and his chest tightened at the trusting gesture. "What do you wish, Beth?"

"That it wasn't over," she said simply.

He cringed inwardly. Her words were uncannily close to the truth—it was, indeed, almost over. But for tonight.

"It's not over," he murmured, brushing his thumb slowly across her bottom lip. "We have tonight. I've planned something special."

"Something special," she repeated breathlessly, a smile tugging at her mouth. "What?"

"A surprise." He sensed her questions, but he bent his head and brushed his mouth against hers before she could voice them. She melted into him, inviting him to go deeper, to taste more. He fought the urge to wrap his arms around her, fought the desire to take her up on her invitation.

When it came to Beth, right and wrong blurred, then melted away; plans became vague, then disappeared. Fact and fabrication became unclear—and unimportant.

That he wanted her was no fabrication. Of that he was certain.

Why, when he was with her, did he find it so difficult to remember the kind of woman she was?

Chance broke the kiss and straightened. "I've got some things to take care of," he said, his voice thick. "I'll have a cab call for you at seven-thirty. Will that give you enough time to get ready?"

She nodded, but instead of dropping her hands, she pressed them against his chest. "Where's your room?"

"Just next door."

She nodded again and stepped away from him.

Calling himself a fool for wanting to pull her back into his arms, he started down the hall. When he reached his door, he turned back to her. "See you tonight."

She lifted her hand in acknowledgment, but didn't make a move to go into her own room. After he'd closed his own door, he leaned against it. If he looked out into the hall now, would she still be standing there, that same vulnerable, wanting look in her eyes? And if so, would he be able to resist the urge to take her into his arms and hold her forever?

Deriding himself for his answer, he set about completing his plans for their evening. And his revenge.

Two hours later, plans complete and revenge at hand, Chance stood in front of the warehouse he'd rented, waiting for her. He checked his watch for the fifth time in as many minutes, cursing the way the seconds seemed to creep.

Tonight was the night. Tonight she would either admit what she'd done or he would confront her with it. Either way, this time she was the one being played for the fool.

He should be pleased. He should feel satisfaction. Yet instead of pleasure, he felt a hollow ache in the vicinity of his heart. Instead of satisfaction, he felt . . . sadness.

Chance scowled. Although he'd long ago learned to suspect motives, he had trusted her. He had grown to like her.

Like? His chest tightened, just a bit, and he swore. What a tame word to describe his feelings for Beth Waters. She made him feel alive and whole and . . .

She made him *feel.*

Only because of his parents, he rationalized. Her manipulation had brought back the pain of his childhood, the disillusionment. The feeling of being torn in two. For even as he stood waiting for Beth, he felt as if he were being wrenched into a dozen different pieces.

Headlights sliced across the dark parking lot. Beth. Finally. Anticipation trembled through him, and the breath eased from his lungs as if he'd been holding it forever.

The cab pulled to a stop; Chance crossed to the door and opened it for her. Beth stepped out, wearing a soft knit crop top and skirt, the color a deep, velvety plum. The sweater buttoned up the front, and the tiny gold buttons shimmered in the soft light. The shawl around her shoulders was made of a filmy transparent material, and he couldn't help thinking of the way it would look draped over her nude body.

Arousal pulsed through him. He reminded himself of what she'd done, that she was the kind of woman who lied and manipulated. He told himself that this seduction was an illusion only, a scene set up to trap her. Making love was not a part of his plan.

He found himself smiling anyway.

"Pier twelve?" she murmured, looking up at the sign, then down at the row of obviously deserted warehouses. She lifted her gaze back to his. "What is this?"

"It's the surprise," he murmured. "Come."

He linked their fingers and led her inside. The huge warehouse was empty save for a double row of potted trees laced with twinkling white lights. The trees ran the length of the warehouse, bordering a white runner. At the end of the twinkling runway stood a gazebo, also laced with white lights.

Filled with delight, Beth turned to him. "It's so beautiful, Chance. But why—"

"Shh." He laid a finger gently on her lips and led her down the runway to the gazebo. Spread out on the gazebo floor was a blanket and picnic basket, a bottle of champagne on ice, and small portable tape player.

"I wanted us to be alone," he murmured, unable to take his gaze from her lovely profile. "No waiters. No musicians. Nobody but . . . us."

That word again, Beth thought, shivering. Questions rushed to her tongue, but she fought them back. She would enjoy this moment, she would take what was offered her. Chance's motivation didn't matter, nor did his feelings for Liza.

She sank onto the blanket, curling her legs under her.

"A friend owns this warehouse," he continued, following her down. "He rents it out for parties." Chance popped the champagne, then poured them each a flute of the sparkling wine. He handed her one and pinged his glass against hers. "I was lucky that it was available."

"Are we celebrating?" she asked.

"Could be."

"The Summer Show?"

"Could be." He sipped his wine and looked at her over the rim of his glass. "You left your hair down."

"Yes." She pushed at the unruly waves, enjoying the way they brushed against her cheeks. Over the last weeks, she'd found she liked wearing her hair down, just as she'd found she like wearing clothes with color and style.

"Are you hungry?"

She was, but not for food. She nodded anyway.

He opened the basket and begun unpacking their feast. "Boiled shrimp on ice. Pâté and crackers, crusty French bread and Brie, petits fours and chocolate-dipped strawberries."

"What?" she teased. "No fried chicken?"

Chance laughed. "Sorry." He spread some pâté on a cracker and handed it to her.

She took a bite. "Mmm, delicious."

Chance fed her another and another, then sampled some of delicacies himself. Through it all he couldn't take his eyes off her. He enjoyed the way she licked her lips and fingers, enjoyed the way she murmured her appreciation at a new texture or flavor.

Would she be as open making love? he wondered. Would she murmur her appreciation? Would she tell him with—and without—words when his mouth or his hands pleasured her?

Beth bit into a strawberry, and the juices pooled on her lips, red and wet. Arousal, sweet and stunning, took his breath. He turned away from her, working for control. He pressed the Play button on the tape deck, and Bing Crosby's "White Christmas" filled the silence around them.

Beth laughed, charmed and delighted. She looked at Chance, words of love flying to her tongue. She swallowed them—barely—but let the emotion shine from her eyes. "You remembered."

Warmth swelled inside him, and, uncomfortable, he lowered his eyes. This wasn't going as he'd planned. The mood was softer, his feelings gentler. He tried to remind himself why they were here, of the things he'd planned to say to trap her, but all he could think of was the blue of her eyes, the rose of her softly parted mouth. The way his own heart hammered in his chest.

"When I was a little girl," she said, tipping her head to the canopy of lights above them, "I was a hopeless daydreamer. My parents worried over it and discouraged it. If they caught me, they would punish me." She laughed lightly. "My favorite fairy tale was Rapunzel."

"I didn't know they had castles in Kansas."

She blushed. "Oh, sure. And towers in which to lock up misunderstood redheaded princesses."

He laughed and eased onto his side on the blanket, propping himself up on an elbow. "You're a romantic."

"Was," she corrected, meeting his gaze, then looking away. "I fashioned all manner of romantic moments and scenarios. This reminds me of one of them." She ran a finger around the rim of the wine flute. "Silly dreams."

"Why silly?" Her shawl had slipped off her shoulders and pooled on the blanket. He rubbed the filmy fabric between his fingers. "Don't all little girls dream of knights in shining armor and Prince Charming?"

"I suppose so." She shrugged. "But I stopped a long time ago."

Even as she murmured the words she realized they were a lie: all along she had wished Chance to be her knight in shining armor, her Prince Charming.

"Because of your parents?" He let the delicate, shimmering fabric slither through his fingers.

"No." Her cheeks heated more, and she lowered her eyes. "For other . . . obvious reasons."

"Obvious to who? Not to me."

"You're being nice."

Is that what she called what he was doing? Being nice? Being captivated was a much better description. Mesmerized would also do.

Chance reached across the blanket and covered her hands with his. "I'm never that nice. Come on, Red. Spill it."

Beth looked down at their joined hands, then back up at him. "All right. I realized pretty quickly that no Prince Charming was going to come after me. I decided to stop setting myself up for disappointment by fantasizing about what I'd never have."

Chance frowned. "Why no Prince Charming?"

She made a sound of frustration and embarrassment. "I have eyes. And so, unfortunately, did the boys. You get to a certain age, and you have to stop kidding yourself. In addition to being plain, I was shy. I didn't know how to flirt or tease. I couldn't even have a conversation with a boy without stammering like a total idiot. I still can't, if you haven't noticed."

As she said the words, he realized that once upon a time he would have described her in such a way. But no more. "You're doing pretty well right now."

Tears sprang to her eyes, and she made a move to stand.

Chance stopped her. He tumbled her down onto the blanket so she sprawled out beside him. He cupped her cheek and searched her expression. The tears that sparkled in her eyes pulled at him, as did her silent shudder of pleasure. "All those things are past tense, Beth. All of them."

She looked away and he swore silently. With a gentleness that took him by surprise, Chance eased her onto her back. Placing his arms on either side of her head, he forced her to meet his eyes.

"Do you remember the night of Artful Fools?" he asked, his voice thick.

How could she have forgotten? It had been the most wonderful night of her life. "Yes," she whispered.

"You were so beautiful. So alluring. That night was so . . . special. I haven't been able to forget it. Or you, Beth." Even as he spoke the words, he wished they were lies. He wished he had been able to forget. And now his thoughts of revenge skittered away, replaced by other, softer thoughts. By other needs, other feelings. Ones that couldn't be pushed away, wouldn't be denied.

She shook her head. "It was the dress."

"No." He leaned down and brushed his mouth against hers. Her lips trembled, whether with uncertainty or passion, he wasn't sure. He tasted her mouth again, this time diving deeper. She caught her breath. The tiny sound, one of both surprise and pleasure, warmed him immeasurably.

He lifted his head. "Not the dress, Beth."

Blood thrummed crazily through her veins. She wanted this, wanted him, more than she'd ever wanted anything. That he desired her was almost incomprehensible to her. She'd never been attractive to men, had never been aroused enough to forget sanity or even good sense.

She'd never been with a man for those reasons.

But now, good sense seemed a laughable illusion, sanity a stifling cloak. She wanted Chance no matter the consequences. She wanted him to stroke and excite and awaken. She wanted to be a woman at last. Chance's woman.

"It was the night," she whispered, reaching up and touching his mouth with her fingertips. "The ocean . . . the food . . . the magical atmosphere."

"No . . ." He caught her fingers and kissed each one, slowly, lingeringly. "No . . ." He kissed her palms, scraping his teeth over the sensitive flesh. "And no."

Beth opened her mouth to protest; he covered hers with his. He found her tongue and stroked with his own, exciting, taking both their breaths.

When he broke the contact, it took a moment for him to find his voice. "Do you remember what happened at my house . . . after the ball?" She nodded shyly, color flooding her cheeks. "When you put my hands on your breasts . . ." He moved his hands now, so that they skimmed the sides of her breasts. She arched her back, a small moan escaping her lips.

"I wanted you so much, I thought I would die," he murmured, moving his hands some more until they cupped her. Her nipples hardened under his palms, and this time it was he who bit back a moan. "But you were right, I was afraid. Because *you* were the magic, Beth. You still are."

Beth pulled his head to hers and caught his mouth, then his tongue. Arousal, stunning in its intensity, swept over her. She pressed herself against him, wrapping her arms around his neck.

She opened her mouth more, her desire laced with desperation. She had tonight. Tomorrow they would return to L.A., to reality. And to the truth. After that, in all probability, she would never see him again.

Pain at the thought arced through her, and she pushed the thought, and the pain, resolutely away. Tomorrow there would be plenty of time for pain, for regrets, and what ifs.

But not tonight. Tonight was for making dreams and illusions a reality.

Beth slipped her hands underneath his sweater and stroked his chest, reveling in the way he felt under her palms—hard and angular. The differences between his body and hers weren't subtle, and she gloried in them. Man was the other part of woman, this man the other part of her. Tonight, for the first time in her life, she would be whole.

Chance tore his mouth from hers, yanked his sweater over his head and threw it aside. Delighted, Beth ran her hands over him, exploring with hands and eyes. He was beautiful. His muscled chest was lightly furred, his flesh hot, as if he burned with fever. She pressed her mouth to his flat nipple. It pebbled under her tongue, and when she nipped, he sucked in a sharp breath.

She'd pleasured him, Beth thought, dizzy with her own power. She moved her mouth to the opposite nipple, pleasuring again.

Chance groaned and dragged her face back to his. Tangling his fingers in her hair, he gazed at her. "Do you know what you're doing to me?" he rasped.

Beth nodded. "I . . . think so."

He tightened his fingers in her hair. "I want us to make love."

Suddenly afraid, Beth searched his gaze. Women from the beginning of time had faced this moment. And lived through it. Chance would be gentle, she knew. He would care for her body, he would cherish her—if only for this night.

She wanted him. And she wanted to know.

"Yes," Beth whispered, arching against him. "Oh, yes, Chance. Make love to me."

Without waiting for further invitation, he began to unbutton her sweater. Impatient, she tried to help; he pushed her fingers away, working the tiny buttons through their holes. When he'd slipped the last one through, he almost reverently parted the fabric.

Her skin glowed white and felt like satin. Her breasts, encased in a lacy brassiere, rose and fell with her labored breathing.

Chance made a sound of pleasure, and their eyes met. "You're beautiful, Red."

Reaching out, he eased the sweater from her shoulders; the fabric slid down her arms, and she shook it off. His fingers barely brushed her skin, and she shuddered at feathery caress, the sensation erotic. With his index finger he hooked a bra strap and, as gently as he had her top, eased it over one shoulder, then the other.

A moment later she was nude before his eyes, trembling with desire. He trailed his fingers over her. A fine sheen of gooseflesh raced after his fingers. Her breasts peaked, and he lowered his head and caught the peak in his mouth. She arched against him, pressing herself closer.

"Beth . . . Beth . . ." He moved his mouth to the opposite breast and, as she had done to him, laved and then nipped.

She thought she would go mad with wanting. She ached, she burned. She moved her fingers to his belt buckle, fumbling in her haste. Again, he pushed her hands aside, only this time it was because she went too slow.

Panting, they kicked off shoes. She shimmied out of her hosiery, he out of his denims. They pushed impatiently at concealing garments; fabric groaned, then eased. Chance tumbled her to the blanket, covering her nude body with his own. She'd never before felt the weight of a man over her, and her breath caught at the sensation. Flesh against flesh, soft against hard, smooth against rough. Earthy and elemental and exciting, it felt so very right.

Chance caught her mouth, then her tongue. His arousal was hard and insistent; hers was just as insistent, but wet and yielding. He moved his hips; she shifted her legs in invitation. He thrust into her.

She gasped in pain and dug her fingers into his shoulders.

Chance stilled, then stiffened, shock rippling over him. *It couldn't be.* He propped himself up on his elbows and looked down at her, at the tears trembling on her lashes, at the truth in her eyes. *It couldn't be—but it was.*

The possibility that she was a virgin had never entered his mind. It changed everything. He didn't know why, but it did.

Chance began to pull away from her, and she tightened her fingers, holding him to her. Pleading without words for him not to stop.

"Beth, I—"

"No." The word shuddered past her lips, and she caught his mouth. Wrapping her legs tighter around him, she moved her hips, forcing him back inside her.

He groaned. "Beth . . . God, do you know what you're doing?"

"Yes." She met his gaze and tightened her legs. "Make love to me, Chance. I want you. And I want to know." She moved her hips again. "Teach me."

He fought for control, knowing that he wanted her too much to refuse her. And knowing also he must move slowly and gently, or he would hurt her.

He lowered his mouth to hers, finding it open and wanting, and kissed her deeply. Stroking his tongue against hers, he imitated the dance they would do with other parts of their bodies, showing her how good it would be.

"Come with me, Red," he murmured against her ear, his skin growing slick with the effort of control. He eased them onto their sides, slipping from her.

Beth whimpered and arched against him; he forced her to go slowly, to savor. He ran his hands over the curve of her hip, the dip of her abdomen—caressing, exciting. Then he explored lower, his palms easing over her thighs, massaging, loosening muscles until she was liquid beneath his hands. He roamed further. She gasped and tried to close her thighs, but he coaxed her with soft, hot words, with movements softer, hotter still. She opened to him.

He found her hot and wet and ready. Even though he burned, he didn't rush. He wanted her to know complete pleasure before he took his. He moved his fingers until her breath came in small gasps, until she arched and shuddered against him.

As she cried out in release, he rolled her onto her back. Slowly, carefully, he eased into her, catching her wince, stroking her inside and out. For long moments he held her, letting her become accustomed to him. His own breath came quickly, his muscles aching from the effort needed to maintain control.

Chance tangled his fingers in her hair. "Are you okay?" he whispered against her trembling mouth.

She blushed. "Yes."

"Good. Now, hold on." He laced their fingers and

thrust; she made a sound of pleasure and pain. He paused, then thrust again; this time she made a sound of pleasure only. With the next thrust she wrapped her legs around him, too impatient for slowly, too hungry to wait.

Chance's control snapped and he made a sound low in his throat, male and feral. The sound hummed over her, making her feel completely woman, totally wanted.

Beth moved her hands over his shoulders, down his sweat-slickened back to cup him. Holding back for her had cost him. Dearly. She felt in the way his muscles quivered with tension beneath her fingers, heard it in his labored breathing, sensed it in the almost desperate way he moved inside her now.

Even as tenderness rippled over her, it was replaced by breathlessness. Then oblivion. Chance found her mouth, catching her sounds of pleasure. As she caught his.

Afterward they rocked together slowly, gently, finishing the way they had begun. Seconds became moments, then minutes. Hearts slowed, breathing evened, flesh cooled.

Still connected, Chase eased them to their sides. Silently they regarded each other. Even as worries and regrets raced into her head, Beth pushed them away. She wouldn't waste this wonderful moment, wouldn't throw it away on second thoughts.

But still, she wished she knew his thoughts, his innermost feelings. She searched his expression. Earlier she'd lied to herself. It mattered very much what his motivation was tonight. It mattered so much, it felt as if she were being ripped apart.

Beth shivered, and Chance draped her shimmery shawl over them. "What are you thinking?" she asked.

"How can you even ask?" He smiled and touched the tip of her nose.

Her heart lurched at the innocence—and intimacy—of the gesture. "Was I . . . was it all right for you?"

"Yes." He eased her onto her back and gazed down at her. Her hair circled her head like a halo of fire. He rubbed some of the strands between his fingers. Soft and silky, they glowed against his fingertips.

The hair of a wayward angel, he thought, not for the first time. He tangled his fingers in the silky mass, feeling like a fraud for wanting her to the exclusion of all else. For forgetting everything he knew about her, for forgetting every lesson of his childhood.

What the hell was he going to do now?

He stiffened, and Beth caught her breath. She saw the regrets that raced into his eyes. He was moving away from her already. She pressed her hands to his chest. "Don't," she said. "Don't be sorry. Not again."

How could he not be? And how could this feel so right anyway? He looked down at her and smiled solemnly. "Was it all right for you?"

"It was wonderful."

"You're not sore?"

She shook her head, then moved and winced. "Maybe a little."

Frowning, he rubbed her hair between his fingers again. "How did it happen, Beth? How was it that you were still a—"

"Virgin," she finished for him. She lowered her eyes for a moment, then lifted them back to his. "I could have . . . you know, a couple of times. But I couldn't go through with it. It felt wrong to do it, just to . . . do it. I didn't really care about either of the men. So—" She drew in a shaky breath. "So here I am, embarrassing but true, the last virgin in America."

"Was." He whispered, brushing his mouth against hers, irrationally pleased to be her first, feeling incredibly macho. "Things have changed in the last hour."

She blushed again, and he skimmed his fingers over her hot cheeks. "I once wondered if you blushed everywhere as deliciously as you do in your cheeks." He raked his gaze slowly and deliberately over her. "You do."

The blushed deepened, and he laughed. "We should go back."

Beth thought of her lonely hotel room and wanted to cry. Tonight was almost over. Her life, and everything about her, had been changed. And yet nothing had changed—for her lie was still between them.

"Yes," she murmured in a subdued voice.

"Hey, what's wrong?"

"I don't want tonight to be over," she whispered, knowing she revealed too much but already too exposed to care.

He smiled tenderly. "Did you think I would just drop you at your door? Do you really think, after what we shared, that I could?"

Her eyes told all, and he muttered an oath and dragged her against his chest. "I don't want this night to end either." He wished he spoke lies, but he did not. He wished he felt nothing, but instead he felt everything—deeply and to the core. "I'm as involved as you are."

He cupped her face in his palms. "I want you to come back to the hotel with me. I want you to come to my room, spend the night with me, in my bed and in my arms."

She drew in a deep, shuddering breath. "Do you mean you want to . . . make love again?"

"Red . . . Red . . ." Chance laughed and hugged her to him. "If I had the capacity, I would make love to you a hundred more times tonight. I have the want . . . Lord, do I have the want."

She laughed with him. "Let's hurry, Chance. Because I have the want too."

Nine

They did hurry. They tugged on their clothes, and after Chance made sure the warehouse was secure, they raced to Chance's rental car. They made it back to the hotel and up to their rooms in record time. At least, it seemed so to Beth.

"I need some things," she said breathlessly, stopping at her door.

Chance nodded, then caught her to him, lowering his mouth to hers in a deep, shattering kiss. "Don't take too long."

Beth let herself into her room, then ran through, collecting the items she needed—her gown and robe, hairbrush and toothbrush, pausing only long enough to dab perfume behind her ears and between her breasts.

As she started for the door, she saw that her message light was blinking. She hesitated, then shook her head. If it was Eva with an emergency, she would try Chance's room as well. Anything else could wait.

Chance opened his door the moment she knocked. Without preamble, she moved into his arms.

"What took so long?" he asked, kissing her lips, her cheeks, her eyebrows. "I thought I would go mad waiting for you."

She laughed and twined her arms around his neck, returning his ardent kisses. "I could grow to like driving you mad."

Chance growled next to her ear and kicked the door shut behind them. "I think you already do, vixen."

Cupping her derriere, he lifted her and she wrapped her legs around his middle. He carried her to the bed, then, still joined, lowered them to the mattress.

"Now," he murmured, his voice thick. "For lesson number two."

They spent the night making love. Lying next to each other, neither was able to sleep for long, and the night took on the quality of an erotic dream.

The first time Chance awakened her, he caressed her with his hands and mouth, arousing, exciting. Tasting places that made her cry out with pleasure, touching her in ways that made her delirious with need.

He dominated and led her, and Beth clutched the sheets in an attempt to anchor herself to the real world. That she could experience such pleasure had been inconceivable to her. Until this night. Until Chance. As sensations skyrocketed through her, she cried out and drew him inside her.

The next time, it was Beth who awakened him; she who explored and ignited, she who led. She proved herself an excellent pupil, for this time it was Chance who clutched the bedding for support, Chance who cried out his release.

So the night went, until exhausted and sated, they both slept.

The next morning Beth awakened slowly. She

became aware of several things simultaneously: the light that pricked the back of her eyelids, the weight of Chance's arm across her chest, the sweet sting of muscles she hadn't even known she had.

Beth moaned and shifted. Her body ached, her limbs felt heavy, her head fuzzy. She found the combination delicious.

Even as sleep beckoned her back, Beth blinked her eyes, gazing at the brilliant sunlight peeking in from behind the heavy drapes. Moving carefully, Beth shimmied from under Chance's arm so she could see the bedside clock.

They had just under two hours before they needed to be at the gallery.

She smiled. Enough time for her to take a minute to savor this time with Chance. To gaze at him. To revel in the fact that, for this moment, he was hers.

Beth shifted again, propping herself up on an elbow, gazing down at him. He was so handsome, she thought, tenderness welling in her chest. And such a good lover. She blushed, thinking of the things he had done to her body, of the things she'd done to his.

Who had that woman been? she wondered. How had she gone from naive to wanton in one night?

Chance. She trusted and loved him. She had opened to him like a flower to the sun. No other man could have touched her so, no other man could have broken through her barriers of shyness and fear.

Beth shook her head in wonder and reached out and touched the arch of one of his dark eyebrows. Was he dreaming? she mused. And if so, was he dreaming of her?

He moaned in his sleep and wiggled his nose. Beth snatched her hand back, insecurity and doubts barreling through her. What would today bring?

This morning they would go to the gallery and finalize plans for the Summer Show, then head home.

Home. She caught her bottom lip between her teeth. And the truth.

Fear trembled through her. She tried to push it away, but it wouldn't be quelled. It clawed at her until her heart raced and her breath came in short, quick gasps.

At this rate she would wake him. And he would see her fear, her uncertainty; he would have questions. Questions she didn't want to answer—not yet.

Beth climbed quietly out of the bed, holding her breath as he muttered something and turned over. She slipped into her gown and robe, then collected her things. After peeking out at the hallway to make sure it was deserted, she raced to her room.

As Beth ducked through the door, paper crackled beneath her feet. She stooped to pick up the hotel envelope, her name and room number printed neatly on its front. Drawing her eyebrows together in question, she ripped it open.

From Eva, the message read: *You've been a very bad girl! Call me.*

Beth stared at the message, heat climbing her cheeks. How had Eva found out about her and Chance's night together? Was her grandmother psychic?

Even as embarrassment took her breath, Beth shook her head. Her grandmother was not a psychic. Eva's message referred to the fact that Beth hadn't called her as she'd promised she would.

Sure.

But still . . .

A trembling sensation in the pit of her stomach, Beth looked at the phone, then the bedside clock.

Eva wouldn't be up yet; this message was nothing—certainly not enough to wake her grandmother over.

Then why did she feel this burning urgency to call her grandmother? Why did she have the feeling that her world was about to fall apart?

Calling herself a neurotic, insecure idiot, Beth crossed to the phone. She would make the call and prove to herself that the message really was nothing. She picked up the phone and punched out Eva's number, her fingers shaking so badly, she had to redial twice.

Raphael answered on the sixth ring. "Beth?" he said groggily after her greeting. "Where are you? San Francisco?"

"That's right," Beth managed, despite her pounding heart. "I'm returning Eva's call. Is she there?"

"Yeah." He yawned into the receiver. "I'll get her. By the way, congrats, kiddo, I couldn't have been happier when I heard the news. Hold on."

Congratulations? News? "Raph, wait—"

Beth bit back the words and a sound of frustration. He'd already put the phone down and gone in search of Eva. A moment later her grandmother picked up. "Darling! I had to hear the news from Raphael? I can't believe you didn't call before this."

"Eva, I just got your message and—"

"Just got my message? My, my." The older woman laughed. "I knew this would happen. And I couldn't be more delighted. Didn't I tell you to trust me? Didn't I tell you everything would work out?"

"Eva, stop!" Beth worked to calm herself. "What are you talking about?"

Her grandmother paused. "Why, the Summer Show, of course. The gallery director told Raph that you were it."

"Me?" Beth repeated, confused. She clutched the

phone cord so tightly, her fingers went numb. "That's impossible."

"How late were you out last night?" Eva made a clucking sound. "Of course it's not impossible. It's a fact. You're the Summer Show's launch artist."

Feeling as if she'd been punched squarely in the chest, Beth's breath hissed from her lungs. "You mean Liza's the launch artist."

"No. The director told Raph the artist's name was Elizabeth Waters."

Beth sank to the bed, the truth rocketing through her. Chance knew. He had known last night. He had known for some time.

"Why didn't you tell me you and Chance had talked? This is the most exciting news. You, the launch artist—"

"Eva . . . I . . . we . . . didn't—" Her words caught on a sob, a wave of devastation overtaking her. "I have to go."

Beth dropped the receiver back into its cradle, then brought her shaking hands to her face.

Chance knew. For how long, she couldn't guess. It didn't matter now. All that mattered was that everything they had shared had been a lie. Beth dropped her hands and stared blankly at the wall, a dozen different emotions tumbling through her, not the least of which were betrayal and shame.

Tears welled in her eyes, then slid down her cheeks. What had last night been about? The whole scene— the intimate picnic, the twinkling lights, the Christmas music.

She caught her breath on a racking sob as she realized the truth. It had been a scene, all right. One set up to punish her. To teach her a lesson.

Lesson number two.

His words rang in her head, cruelly mocking her.

She'd been such a fool. A starry-eyed idiot. Wrapping her arms around herself, she doubled over, the sound that wrenched from inside her bitter and hollow and hurting. Why hadn't she suspected or questioned? She'd been so stupid. So . . . trusting.

Beth swiped at the tears on her cheeks. How could she have thought that suddenly he had been interested in her? In plain, mousy Beth Waters. In the woman no man before had been interested in, let alone a man as attractive and worldly as Chance Michaels? He'd called her sexy. Alluring. She had believed him so easily. Because she had wanted to so badly.

What a great laugh he must have had at her expense.

It hurt so much, she thought she might die.

Don't let him get away with it.

The thought threaded through her pain and devastation, and she rubbed her hands over her tear-streaked face. Don't let him get away with it, she thought again, fighting a wave of fear and denial. Her every instinct screamed for her to run and hide, to spare herself the agony of seeing him again. Spare herself looking into his eyes and knowing that what they'd shared had been nothing but a vicious payback.

Beth stood. Two months ago she would have followed her instincts and done just that. Two months ago, because of her fears, she'd created the charade that had gotten her into this mess.

She inched her trembling chin up. She'd changed. Just as she had planned to face him with her own lie, she would face him with his.

She wouldn't run. She would never run again.

Beth showered, scrubbing her body and hair, attempting to remove all traces of Chance from her person. But she couldn't scrub away the ache in her muscles, and each time she moved she was reminded of their night together and the lie of his lovemaking.

Nor could she wash away the pain in her heart.

She dressed, then packed. Using the mundane chore to help calm herself, she neatly hung and folded her clothes. She managed to ignore the way her hands shook, but couldn't ignore the quiver of hysteria hovering just at the edge of her calm.

How was she going to face Chance without falling apart?

Her packing finished, Beth took a deep breath. Get it over with, she told herself. Then move on. After taking one last look at her sterile hotel room, she let herself out of it and headed to his.

Chance answered before she'd even finished knocking. She took one look at him and her hard-fought control crumbled. She saw relief in his eyes. And a lingering alarm. He'd showered and dressed, yet something in his expression still looked sleepy and sated.

"Beth, thank God. I was worried."

He swung open the door, and she brushed past him without speaking. A cry flew to her throat as she saw the bed, as she realized the room smelled of their lovemaking. She choked back the cry and turned slowly to face him.

"I missed you," he murmured. "When I woke and saw that you'd gone—"

"When were you going to tell me," she demanded. "When, Chance?"

He drew his eyebrows together in confusion, searching her expression. "Tell you . . . what?"

"When I got back to my room, there was a message from Eva waiting for me. Congratulating me on being the launch artist for the Summer Show." Her voice quivered. "How long have you known?"

Chance stared at her, his confusion becoming fury as he realized what she meant.

"Your indignation is perfect," he murmured. "Just perfect. You are a better actress than your grandmother. The deceiver here is you. You used me to further your art career."

His words took her aback.

"I found out about your little game early on, Beth. Or is it Liza?"

She felt the blood drain from her cheeks. "What do you mean, to further my art?"

Chance continued as if she hadn't spoken. "I saw through your charade at the coffeehouse, although I didn't have my proof until that night in *Liza's* studio. Remember that night? Remember our . . . kiss?" He saw by her expression that she did. "In the heat of the moment, I called you Beth. You didn't notice. I knew then for sure." He shook his head in derision. "You weren't even a good liar, Beth."

She stared at him, remembering all the times between that moment and this one, remembering all the things they'd said to each other. The things they had done. Everything had been a lie.

She wrapped her arms around herself in an attempt to ward off the pain, the feeling of absolute betrayal. *He thought she'd created Liza to further her art career.* She moved her gaze to the bed, still jumbled from their lovemaking. How could he think that little of her? He didn't know her at all.

"When were *you* going to tell *me*?"

"After we got back to L.A. This afternoon." Beth found the words lame even to her own ears, and saw by his expression that he found them so too. "It's true, Chance."

He laughed coldly. "I'm sure it is. You were going to tell me after you found out about the Summer Show."

"No!" She took a step toward him. "What I did wasn't about my . . . art. It was about my fears. My lack of self-confidence. It was about my—"

"What?" he interrupted caustically. "Your love?"

His words cut her to the core. She lifted her chin another notch, determined never again to be the woman who had gone to such ridiculous lengths out of fear. She was done hiding. "Yes."

"Give me a break! I haven't been that dumb since I was thirteen."

"It's true." She drew in a deep breath, desperation tightening in the pit of her stomach. "It started out as a harmless fib—a white lie. You saw my sketches that morning and I couldn't bear for you to know they were mine. I couldn't bear for you to reject them. So . . . I said they were my sister's."

"Your sister," he mimicked. "Do you even have a sister?"

"No." Heat flew to her cheeks. "Liza is the name my grandmother always called me."

The sound he made was harsh. She continued, even though she knew he would never believe her. "Everything I told you about Liza and her art was true. I tried not to lie. As often as I could, I spoke to you from my heart."

She let her words trail off, then stiffened her spine. He would never believe her, but she would have her say anyway. "Without meaning to, I got deeper and deeper into the lie, and I didn't know how to get back out."

"Without telling the truth?"

She lifted her chin. "Without losing you." At his expression, she laughed. "You'd told me about your parents. I knew how you felt about deceit. I couldn't face the thought of never seeing you again."

Chance narrowed his eyes, stealing himself against the emotions raging over and through him. Her words pulled at him, at his heart. He shook his head in denial of them and her. "That was about your art. You saw me as your shot at the big time."

"No." She met his gaze evenly. "I didn't want to lose *you*, Chance. I love you."

He curled his fingers into fists. Just like his parents, she used love to justify her actions. "Convenient, Beth. I'm sure there's some poor slob out there who would believe you, but not me."

She made a sound of anger and frustration, and took a step closer to him. "What I did was wrong, I regretted it from the first and hated lying. But I didn't do it to hurt you. I did it out of fear. First of exposing myself and later of losing you."

She took a deep breath. "You deliberately tried to hurt me, Chance. You set me up. I was a virgin. How could you . . . do that to me?"

The expression in her eyes tore at him, and he spun away from her. "I *had* set up last night to pay you back," he said softly. "To trap you into admitting the truth. But it didn't go that way." He laughed, the sound harsh and hollow and hurting. "I couldn't go through with it."

Couldn't go through with it? Beth clasped her hands in front of her. "Then why . . . what did happen last night?"

He turned and stared at her, furious with her lies and manipulations, but more furious with himself for forgetting about them even if only for a night. Furious that he'd allowed her to touch him. To hurt him.

Once he had felt nothing; now he felt everything. It scared him to death.

"What," she repeated, a thread of hope beginning to curl through her, "happened last night?"

Chance crossed to the window. Softly yet with a leashed violence, he knocked his fist against the window frame. When he turned back to her, the expression in his eyes was as cold and unyielding as the glass behind him. "Sex, Beth. Not planned. Not part of revenge. But nothing more either."

She felt as if he'd slapped her. Why those words, after all the others they had flung at each other, should hurt so badly, she didn't know. But they did.

She worked to find her voice. "I think I hate you now."

For a full ten seconds he stared at her, a muscle jumping in his jaw. Then he narrowed his eyes. "Fine. Good, as a matter of fact. But our business together is far from finished, Elizabeth Waters."

"I wouldn't work with you now even if—"

"Your art . . . Liza. You signed a three-year contract with me. I'm your exclusive West Coast representative. And I'm going to launch your career with the Summer Show."

"I don't care about the show. And I don't want it. You can take your show and—"

"You're it anyway." He hardened his jaw. "Congratulations."

Her breath caught on a sob. "Why are you doing this? You obviously despise me." She thought of the night before and what they'd shared, and her eyes filled with tears. "Why would you want to represent me? Why try to make me a . . . star?"

"It's business," he said without inflection. "You've got star talent. A lot of nice people wouldn't make me a cent. But you"—he raked his gaze over her—"you'll make me a fortune."

She wrapped her arms around herself, her tears brimming, then spilling over. How could he be so cold? And how could she still love him after what he'd done.

"I hope you're happy, Elizabeth Waters. You got what you wanted."

Ten

Beth knocked on her grandmother's door. She'd called the older woman repeatedly over the last day and a half, with no reply. It wasn't like Eva not to return phone messages, and Beth worried that something had happened to her.

Beth pounded again, thinking of the weeks since that last awful scene between her and Chance. Each day had crept by agonizingly, and each day she had told herself that time would heal her, that eventually the pain would be gone and she would be able to breathe evenly again.

But so far the hurt had only worsened, and some days she had wondered how she would survive to face the next.

Thank goodness she'd had her exhibition to concentrate on. Plans for it had catapulted forward, and her days had been filled with getting works framed, then shipped; she'd been in constant touch with the San Francisco gallery and Chance's new assistant at Art One.

Funny how some dreams come true . . . and some didn't.

Beth's eyes filled with tears, and muttering an oath, she blinked them away. If only she *could* hate him. If only she could forget him.

But the truth was, she loved him too much to ever forget him.

Beth pounded on Eva's door again, then pressed her ear to the wood. Fear snaked through her. What would she do if she lost her grandmother too? She didn't think she would be able to go on.

"Eva," she called, this time hammering with her fist on the door. "It's me, Beth. If you're in there, please open up."

A moment later she heard a shuffling sound from inside the apartment, then the click of the lock turning. Beth almost cried out in relief as the door swung open. "Eva, thank God! Where have you been? I was terrified . . ."

Beth's words trailed off. Her grandmother's face was devoid of cosmetics, her eyes red and swollen, her mouth etched as if with years of bitter disappointments. She looked old and beaten.

Stunned, Beth brought a hand to her own mouth. She'd never seen her grandmother this way. Eva had always been ageless, full of life and laughter and spirit. But now . . .

Beth caught her grandmother's hands. "My God, Eva! What's happened? Are you ill?"

"My agent called," her grandmother said. "I didn't get the part. They gave it to the younger actress."

"Oh, Eva . . ." Beth squeezed her hands. "I'm so sorry. I know how badly you wanted that part."

Her grandmother's eyes teared, and she slipped her hands from Beth's. Without another word, she turned and walked slowly to the living room.

Beth followed her, watching as her grandmother sank onto the couch and pulled an afghan around her, huddling into it. It hurt to see her so unhappy, and Beth drew in a shaky breath, wanting to ease the other woman's pain. "There will be other parts, Eva."

She shook her head. "No."

Beth crossed to her, and kneeled down in front of her. "What do you mean, no?" Beth smiled, trying to reassure. "Of course there will be. There's always another part, that's what you've always said."

"That was before I got old." Eva clutched the afghan to her. "Writers create stories about the young. And for the few parts available to someone older, directors hire young talent and have them made up to look old." She shook her head. "No, it's too late for me."

"Don't say that! It's not too late. Didn't you always tell me that a person is only as young—or as old—as she wants to be?" She gripped the other woman's hands. "You came so close this time—you almost had your dream! Next time—"

"No." Eva shook her head again. "Don't you see? I was better than that other actress, but they hired her because she was younger. It's not about talent anymore, it's about something that I can't control or change." She drew in a deep, shaky breath. "The time comes when you have to face the facts. And the facts are—I'm never going to be more than a two-bit, fourth-rate actress. I'm never going to make it."

"That's not true, Eva! It's not." Tears filled Beth's eyes. "You're a wonderful actress. You've wanted other parts. You've never given up when you didn't get them."

"This part was my last chance. It's over, Beth." A solitary tear rolled down Eva's cheek. "I've wasted my life. To the exclusion of all else, I chased my impossible dream. I ruined your mother's childhood, and now I've screwed up your life. If I hadn't pushed you into this Liza thing, if I hadn't cornered you—"

"I wouldn't have a one-person show opening this weekend," Beth interrupted, fear and desperation racing through her. If her grandmother gave up her dream she would wither, then die. If she gave up her dream, she would have nothing to live for. "If you hadn't pushed, I'd still be painting pictures no one would ever see."

"You would have Chance," her grandmother finished sadly. "It's my fault you're so unhappy. Everything's my fault."

"Stop it!" Beth jumped up and faced her grandmother. "First of all, I made my choices, not you. Any mess I'm in, I created." She placed her fists on her hips. "And secondly, how can you say you wasted your life? You've had fun and freedom. You haven't allowed yourself to be ruled by fears or by what others expected of you. You've believed in yourself, Eva. You've had the courage of your own convictions.

"How many people can say that of their lives? How many people can say that they've lived their lives as they wanted?" Beth lowered her voice. "You're my hero, Eva. You showed me how to live, you encouraged me to be confident and courageous. And you always . . . always believed in me. When no one else did, not even me."

Her eyes brimming with tears, Beth knelt back down in front of her grandmother. "If not for you, I would still be trapped in the cloak of fear that was suffocating me. I'm not afraid anymore, Eva. I don't care what anybody thinks about me . . . except me."

As she said the words, Beth realized she meant them. Her whole life she had allowed fears to rule her and others to control her. She'd changed. She was no longer Beth Waters, afraid of her own shadow. She'd become a new woman—a combination of the woman she'd created from her own fantasies and the person she'd been all along.

Beth stared at her stunned grandmother, then laughed with delight. "Eva, you say I'm unhappy—how could I be? For the first time in my life I know what it is to be free and whole." She laughed again and drew the older woman to her feet. "For the first time in my life I'm completely myself! If you hadn't bullied me, it wouldn't have happened."

Beth hugged her, ecstatic with hope, dizzy with her own power. "I'll make Chance love me, Eva. I know I can . . . because he's half in love with me already."

At first Beth thought her grandmother was crying, then she realized she was chuckling. Beth loosened her hold on the other woman, tipping her head back to meet her gaze. As she did, relief rushed over her—the sparkle had returned to her grandmother's eyes. Eva was back and, Beth could tell, already plotting.

"And how do you propose to do that?" Eva asked, arching an eyebrow.

Beth paused, then shook her head. "I don't know. But I'm going to do whatever it takes. For the first time in my life I'm going to put it all—my heart and everything else I am and have—on the line."

"Well, I'm done interfering," her grandmother said regally. "But I suggest something grand."

Beth bit back a smile. "Theatrical even."

"Yes." The older woman began to pace. "Your opening is this weekend. He'll be there?"

"Without a doubt."

"It will be the perfect opportunity."

"My thoughts exactly."

"We'll have to find you just the right dress."

"I'm sure you have something."

Eva stopped pacing and faced her granddaughter. "If all else fails, I'll lock you up together in the storage closet."

Beth grinned. "And I'll seduce him."

"An excellent plan."

"Eva?" Beth smiled as the older woman met her eyes. "Welcome back."

What had he done?

Chance stared down at the publicity photos of Beth on his desk in front of him, the ones they'd used for the Summer Show's press releases. Her image smiled shyly back at him, taunting him for his stupidity. His insides twisted.

He loved her.

There, he'd admitted it. Even if only to himself. He'd fallen in love with Beth . . . and he'd driven her away. How could he have been such a fool?

He lightly caressed the photo's glossy surface, his senses remembering the softness of her skin. He smiled a little, wonder and tenderness warming him. She'd reached beyond the barrier of fear he'd erected around himself and touched him. Deeply and without trying. He would never be the same again.

Still holding her photo, he swiveled his chair around to face the window. It rarely rained in southern California, yet here it was . . . raining. The water sluiced over his picture window, running in rivulets down to drench and nourish the dry and thirsty earth.

As Beth had nourished him. He'd been dying and he hadn't even known it.

Chance looked back down at the photo. She'd sneaked up on him. Her sense of warmth and humor, her intelligence and wit, her sweetness and vulnerability. Her honesty.

Honesty. He thought of that night in her studio, of the expression on her face, of the fear he'd felt emanating from her in almost palpable waves. He remembered her insecurity that day at the coffeehouse, remembered the way she had lifted her chin as if readying herself for a blow.

What she'd told him of her reasons for creating Liza had been the truth. She hadn't meant to hurt him; she hadn't even meant to lie. She'd been terrified of revealing her art and being rejected.

Beth had been emotionally honest all along. It was he who had lied. To her. To himself.

Chance shook his head and gazed out at the gray sky. He'd accused her of playing games, yet his entire life had been a game. The game of hiding from his feelings, of making sure no one got too close. Making sure no one ever had the power to hurt him the way his parents had.

Beth had ended that. She'd gotten so close so fast, it had scared the hell out of him. So he'd played more games, and finally he'd driven her away.

Now he faced the prospect of life without her. Of never holding her again, of never laughing together, never sharing moments of the day-to-day grind. Never making love with her. Pain arced through him, and he grimaced. How could he fear being hurt when he already hurt so badly, he thought he would never be whole again?

Love hadn't ruined his parents' marriage and his childhood. His parents had.

The realization hit him like a blow to his chest. He had wanted someone, something to blame. He hadn't wanted to point the finger at his parents, because he loved them, they'd been his world.

So the child in him had blamed love.

The time had come to let go of childish notions. The time had come to stop letting the past color his present, to stop letting his fears rule him.

Beth. Chance gazed down at her photograph, pain a living thing inside him. He'd been the unfeeling, manipulative bastard. She hated him now; he couldn't blame her. He'd lost her.

He lifted his eyes from her image to his picture window. The rain had stopped and the dark clouds were beginning to part, brilliant sunlight peeking from beyond. Some of the light escaped and tumbled through his window. Taking a deep breath, he reached his hand out to the light, to its brilliant warmth. Despite his actions of late, he wasn't a coward. He certainly wasn't a quitter.

And the measure between love and hate was small indeed.

Chance thought of the hurt in Beth's eyes at their last meeting, of the way her voice had trembled. Then he thought of their lovemaking. She had given herself to him, wholly and with complete trust. She'd loved him. She still did.

But could she forgive him?

There had to be a way, Chance thought, determination and hope colliding inside him. The clouds parted some more, the sunlight fell over him, bathing him in heat. He would see Beth at her opening tonight; he would get her alone and beg her forgiveness. He would coax and court, and if necessary begin back at square one to prove to her he was a changed man. And that he loved her.

Six hours later Chance stood at the edge of the opening-night crowd, watching Beth's progress as she moved through the room. Things were not going according to plan, Chance thought grimly. Because of the crowd clamoring for her attention, not only had he been unable to get her alone, he hadn't even spoken to her.

The show was a huge success, just as he'd known it would be. The press had arrived en masse, as had collectors and the usual art crowd hangers-on. Her paintings had wowed them. She had charmed them. Beth was on her way to becoming an art star.

Chance frowned. And for the first time ever, he didn't give a flip about the show's success. If it hadn't meant so much to her, he would have kicked everybody out before it had even gotten under way.

From across the room he heard her laugh, and his frown deepened. All evening he'd catch her peeking at him from the corner of her eyes, then someone would claim her attention and she'd turn her back to him. He'd vacillated between believing she loved him and believing she hated him. The woman was driving him crazy.

Her dress didn't help. Red, with a short, flirty skirt, it played peekaboo with her knees as she walked, and Chance had found himself following her with his gaze, mesmerized and hoping for a glimpse of creamy skin. The dress's color, especially on a redhead, shouted, "Notice me!"; its soft silky fabric whispered "Touch me."

God, how he wanted to.

Chance tightened his fingers on the stem of his champagne glass as she tipped her head back and laughed at something one of the collectors said to her. Chance narrowed his eyes. The man was as rich as Roosevelt and a notorious womanizer. If he so much as touched Beth, Chance vowed, he'd pulverize him.

As if Beth sensed his appraisal, she turned and looked directly at him. She smiled, the curving of her lips slow and saucy. Then the collector whispered something in her ear and she turned away from him once more.

Chance slammed down his glass, muttered an oath, and began to thread his way through the crowd, ignoring the greetings of the people he passed.

When he reached her, he took her arm. "Excuse us, Malcolm." As the man began to balk, Chance narrowed his eyes in warning. He didn't give a damn if the man was one of the most important collectors in California—Malcolm J. Reynolds was not going to collect his woman.

The other man took a step backward, flushing. "Of course, of course." He turned back to Beth, bending gallantly over her hand. "Au revoir, my dear. Later, perhaps?"

"Perhaps," Beth murmured, biting back a smile at the way Chance glowered at her. She sighed as the collector walked away. "Charming man."

"He's an old lech," Chance said tightly. "Stay away from him."

"My, my," she murmured. "That's rather territorial, isn't it? Was there some fine print in my contract that I missed? Something about who I could choose to spend my time with or date?"

Chance gazed down at her, furious. His shy little virgin had turned into a vixen, and he had no one to blame but himself. He bit back an oath. "You seem to have bounced back remarkably well."

"From what?" she asked.

He wanted to kiss her so badly, he shook. "From me, dammit."

"If I recall correctly, you left me no choice. Remember, I'm just a business opportunity?"

He tightened his fingers on her arm and lowered his voice. "Stop it, Beth."

She tugged against his grasp. "If you'll excuse me, I have collectors to charm."

Instead of releasing her, Chance tumbled her against his chest and lowered his mouth to hers in a bruising kiss. Her head fell back at the pressure of his mouth, and she grabbed his arms for support. Conversation around them came to a halt, then began again in a symphony of delighted whispers.

Chance glared at them all; Beth smiled brilliantly. "You're causing a scene."

"Vultures," he muttered. "No doubt a little juice will help sales."

"I'm doing just fine without 'juice,' as you so elegantly put it. Or haven't you noticed?"

Furious, he turned his narrowed eyes on her. "Believe me, I've noticed plenty tonight. Come on." He began dragging her toward the storage room, the only place he was sure they would be alone.

"What do you think you're doing?" Beth whispered, halfheartedly resisting. "I'm the artist, I can't leave."

"The opening is almost over, and the artist always leaves a fraction before the crowd. It's the way it's done."

"Oh, I see," Beth murmured. "Being dragged from the room by a glowering barbarian is the way it's done."

"Watch it, Red." He tugged her into the storage room and snapped the door shut behind them. "I'm on an extremely short tether."

"Really?" She lifted her eyebrows in mock surprise. "And I thought that was a thundercloud following me around all night."

He glared at her. "Do you want him?"

"Who?"

"Malcolm."

She lifted her chin. "What do you think?"

"You're driving me crazy."

"You deserve it. Now let me go," she said, pushing against his chest.

"Stop it, Beth."

"Why should I?"

"Because I love you, dammit."

Beth looked weakly up at him. "What did you say?"

"I love you."

Beth stared at him. She hadn't expected this. She'd been determined to prove to him he felt something for her, even if only lust. She'd been prepared to take their relationship one step at a time, giving him all the time he needed to fall in love with her.

She caught her breath in disbelieving wonder. *He loved her already?*

He pulled her closer, breathing a sigh of relief when she didn't resist. "I've loved you for a long time, but I was too afraid to see the truth. That's what was going on the night of Artful Fools. You hit it right on the head. I was terrified of being hurt, of feeling the way I had as a child. So I played games. With you. With myself. I closed myself off from emotion. If I didn't allow myself to care; if I didn't let anyone touch me, I couldn't be hurt."

He ran his fingers over her face, absorbing and memorizing everything about her. "Remembering me telling you that I liked children's art because it's so honest, so emotional? It seems so obvious now, I can't believe I didn't see it before. I didn't allow myself to feel, so I surrounded myself with somebody else's feelings. Somebody else's honest emotions."

He smiled. "Then you came along. You forced me

to feel again. You touched me. I couldn't protect myself from you. And it scared the hell out of me. So I pushed you away. Or rather, I tried to push you away. But I couldn't hide my heart, and you had it almost from the first."

"What about . . ." The words caught in her throat. Swallowing her fear, she took a deep breath. "Are you sure it's *me* you love? Not some figment of my own imagination?"

Chance brushed his mouth over hers. "I always wanted to be only with you, Beth. After Artful Fools, I couldn't stop thinking about you. I couldn't eat or sleep, I couldn't concentrate on work. That's damn terrifying for a man who had never let anyone close enough to matter."

He laughed softly. "But I couldn't admit the truth. How could I? Admitting the truth would force me to admit other things I wasn't ready to. So I played games. I used proving a point as a way to be with you."

"Oh, Chance . . ." Beth stroked his cheek. "We were both so afraid of being hurt, we almost lost out on being really happy."

"I always saw the whole you," he whispered. "I always saw the woman who created the paintings out there—images of sensitivity and spirit, of heart and hurt and strength of will. And I love the woman who made me laugh and feel, the woman who made me see how much I needed her."

"I love you so much, Chance."

He caught her mouth, and she wound her arms around his middle, holding him tightly, vowing to never let him go. When he ended the kiss, they were both breathless.

"We should go back out there," he murmured.

Beth pressed against him. "I'd rather stay in here

and make love. I've missed you terribly, I thought I would die from wanting you."

Chance groaned. "And I you. Come here—"

At the knock on the door, they sprang apart guiltily.

"Darlings," Eva called. "I know you're in there. Come out, come out . . . people are talking."

Beth opened the door a crack and frowned out at her grandmother. "Since when have you cared if people talked?"

The older woman stiffened. "I don't mind if people are talking about me. Which is part of the reason I want you out here. I have an announcement."

Chance groaned again; Beth sighed. They reluctantly left their haven. As they stepped back into the showroom, they saw that save for a handful of friends and the gallery personnel, everyone had left. But those still in attendance burst into applause.

Chance colored and threw his hands up. "I love her, okay? We needed to talk."

As the applause died down Eva moved to the center of the room. "May I have your attention, please. I have just learned," she said with dramatic flourish, "that I have been chosen to play Monique on "Park Place." You are all invited to a celebration at Malibu's directly after the opening."

Beth gasped and turned to her grandmother. "What? When did this happen?"

Eva laughed. "After you'd already left for the opening. The actress they hired, the *younger* actress, fell and broke her hip and won't be able to take the part. So . . ." Eva paused for effect. "You are now looking at a television . . . star. I leave for New York in the morning."

"Oh, Eva." Beth hugged her. "I'm so happy for you!"

Eva shrugged nonchalantly. "As I've always said, it's all a matter of believing in yourself. And of following your heart."

As everyone excitedly circled her grandmother, Beth stepped back, giving the older woman the limelight. She met Chance's eyes. Smiling, he held out his hand. She caught it, and they laced their fingers. "I love you," she whispered.

"And I love you. Come here." Tugging on her hand, he drew her against him.

She pressed one hand against his chest, enjoying the steady beat of his heart under her palm. She tipped her head back and smiled up at him. "No more fears."

He shook his head solemnly. "No more fears."

"From now on we follow our hearts."

"Exclusively."

She slid her hands up to his shoulders. "You know what?"

"Hmm?" He tangled his fingers in her hair, rubbing the silky strands between his fingers.

"I think Eva has stolen this show. Which . . ." Standing on tiptoes, Beth pressed her lips to his. ". . . frees us to pursue . . ." She nipped at his ear. ". . . other ventures."

"Such as?" he murmured, moving his hands in slow circles against the small of her back.

She sighed. "The storage room."

"I like the way you think."

"Me too."

Laughing and holding on to each other, they began their life together.

Epilogue

Beth stared down at the letter in her hands, a grin tugging at her mouth. The letter promised all manner of reward and retribution, depending on her response to its demands.

"Mail came?"

Beth turned to smile at Chance, who had poked his head into her studio. "It sure did."

He sauntered across the room, stopping behind her and dropping a kiss on the top of her head. Hands on her shoulders, Chance peeked at the paper she held, reading its contents. "Another chain letter?"

"Mmm-hmm."

"Uh-oh," he teased, "I better run out and buy stamps."

Beth tapped her index finger against her chin, pretending to think it over. "Let's see, last time I got one of these, I pitched it and found true love, my true self, and a professional success I'd been too afraid to even dream of."

Laughing, she tore the letter in two, tossed it in the

trash, and turned to face her husband. "And I don't want you running anywhere."

"No?"

"No." Beth shook her head and grinned wickedly. "I have plans for you right here."

Taking his hand, she led him to their bedroom, where she put her plans into action.

THE EDITOR'S CORNER

Next month LOVESWEPT salutes **MEN IN UNIFORM**, those daring heroes who risk all for life, liberty . . . and the pursuit of women they desire. **MEN IN UNIFORM** are experts at plotting seductive maneuvers, and in six fabulous romances, you'll be at the front lines of passion as each of these men wages a battle for the heart of the woman he loves.

The first of our dashing heroes is Brett Upton in **JUST FRIENDS** by Laura Taylor, LOVESWEPT #600—and he's furious about the attack on Leah Holbrook's life, the attack that cost her her memory and made her forget the love they'd once shared and that he'd betrayed. Now, as he desperately guards her, he dares to believe that fate has given him a second chance to win back the only woman he's ever wanted. Laura will hold you spellbound with this powerful romance.

In **FLYBOY** by Victoria Leigh, LOVESWEPT #601, veteran Air Force pilot Matt Cooper has seen plenty of excitement, but nothing compares to the storm of desire he feels when he rescues Jennifer Delaney from a raging typhoon. Matt has always called the world his home, but the redhead suddenly makes him long to settle down. And with wildfire embraces and whispers of passionate fantasies, he sets out to make the independent beauty share his newfound dream. A splendid love story, told with plenty of Victoria's wit.

Patricia Potter returns to LOVESWEPT with **TROUBA-DOUR,** LOVESWEPT #602. Connor MacLaren is fiercely masculine in a kilt—and from the moment she first lays eyes on him, Leslie Turner feels distinctly overwhelmed. Hired as a publicist for the touring folk-singer, she'd expected anything except this rugged Scot who awakens a reckless hunger she'd never dare confess. But armed with a killer grin and potent kisses, Connor vows to make her surrender to desire. You'll treasure this enchanting romance from Pat.

In her new LOVESWEPT, **HART'S LAW,** #603, Theresa Gladden gives us a sexy sheriff whose smile can melt steel. When Johnny Hart hears that Bailey Asher's coming home, he remembers kissing her breathless the summer she was seventeen—and wonders if she'd still feel so good in his embrace. But Bailey no longer trusts men and she insists on keeping her distance. How Johnny convinces her to open her arms—and heart—to him once more makes for one of Theresa's best LOVESWEPTs.

SURRENDER, BABY, LOVESWEPT #604 by Suzanne Forster, is Geoff Dias's urgent message to Miranda Witherspoon. A soldier of fortune, Geoff has seen and done it all, but nothing burns in his memory more than that one night ten years ago when he'd tasted fierce passion in Miranda's arms. When he agrees to help her find her missing fiancé, he has just one objective in mind: to make her see they're destined only for each other. The way Suzanne writes, the sexual sparks practically leap off the page!

Finally, in **HEALING TOUCH** by Judy Gill, LOVESWEPT #605, army doctor Rob McGee needs a wife to help him raise his young orphaned niece—but what he wants is

Heather Tomasi! He met the lovely temptress only once two years before, but his body still remembers the silk of her skin and the wicked promises in her eyes. She's definitely not marriage material, but Rob has made up his mind. And he'll do anything—even bungee jump—to prove to her that he's the man she needs. Judy will delight you with this wonderful tale.

On sale this month from FANFARE are four fabulous novels. From highly acclaimed author Deborah Smith comes **BLUE WILLOW,** a gloriously heart-stopping love story with characters as passionate and bold as the South that brought them forth. Artemas Colebrook and Lily MacKenzie are bound to each other through the Blue Willow estate . . . and by a passion that could destroy all they have struggled for.

The superstar of the sensual historical, Susan Johnson tempts you with **SINFUL.** Set in the 1780s, Chelsea Ferguson must escape a horrible fate—marriage to a man she doesn't love—by bedding another man. But Sinjin St. John, Duke of Seth, refuses to be her rescuer and Chelsea must resort to a desperate deception that turns into a passionate adventure.

Bestselling LOVESWEPT author Helen Mittermeyer has penned **THE PRINCESS OF THE VEIL,** a breathtakingly romantic tale set in long-ago Scotland and Iceland. When Viking princess Iona is captured by the notorious Scottish chief Magnus Sinclair, she vows never to belong to him, though he would make her his bride.

Theresa Weir, author of the widely praised **FOREVER,** delivers a new novel of passion and drama. In **LAST SUMMER,** movie star Johnnie Irish returns to his Texas hometown, intent on getting revenge. But all thoughts of getting even disappear when he meets the beautiful widow Maggie Mayfield.

Also on sale this month in the hardcover edition from Doubleday is **SACRED LIES** by Dianne Edouard and Sandra Ware. In this sexy contemporary novel, Romany Chase must penetrate the inner sanctum of the Vatican on a dangerous mission . . . and walk a fine line between two men who could be friend or foe.

Happy reading!

With warmest wishes,

Nita Taublib

Nita Taublib
Associate Publisher
LOVESWEPT and FANFARE

OFFICIAL RULES TO WINNERS CLASSIC SWEEPSTAKES

No Purchase necessary. To enter the sweepstakes follow instructions found elsewhere in this offer. You can also enter the sweepstakes by hand printing your name, address, city, state and zip code on a 3" x 5" piece of paper and mailing it to: Winners Classic Sweepstakes, P.O. Box 785, Gibbstown, NJ 08027. Mail each entry separately. Sweepstakes begins 12/1/91. Entries must be received by 6/1/93. Some presentations of this sweepstakes may feature a deadline for the Early Bird prize. If the offer you receive does, then to be eligible for the Early Bird prize your entry must be received according to the Early Bird date specified. Not responsible for lost, late, damaged, misdirected, illegible or postage due mail. Mechanically reproduced entries are not eligible. All entries become property of the sponsor and will not be returned.

Prize Selection/Validations: Winners will be selected in random drawings on or about 7/30/93, by VENTURA ASSOCIATES, INC., an independent judging organization whose decisions are final. Odds of winning are determined by total number of entries received. Circulation of this sweepstakes is estimated not to exceed 200 million. Entrants need not be present to win. All prizes are guaranteed to be awarded and delivered to winners. Winners will be notified by mail and may be required to complete an affidavit of eligibility and release of liability which must be returned within 14 days of date of notification or alternate winners will be selected. Any guest of a trip winner will also be required to execute a release of liability. Any prize notification letter or any prize returned to a participating sponsor, Bantam Doubleday Dell Publishing Group. Inc.. its participating divisions or subsidiaries, or VENTURA ASSOCIATES, INC. as undeliverable will be awarded to an alternate winner. Prizes are not transferable. No multiple prize winners except as may be necessary due to unavailability, in which case a prize of equal or greater value will be awarded. Prizes will be awarded approximately 90 days after the drawing. All taxes, automobile license and registration fees, if applicable, are the sole responsibility of the winners. Entry constitutes permission (except where prohibited) to use winners' names and likenesses for publicity purposes without further or other compensation.

Participation: This sweepstakes is open to residents of the United States and Canada, except for the province of Quebec. This sweepstakes is sponsored by Bantam Doubleday Dell Publishing Group, Inc. (BDD), 666 Fifth Avenue, New York, NY 10103. Versions of this sweepstakes with different graphics will be offered in conjunction with various solicitations or promotions by different subsidiaries and divisions of BDD. Employees and their families of BDD, its division, subsidiaries, advertising agencies, and VENTURA ASSOCIATES, INC., are not eligible.

Canadian residents, in order to win, must first correctly answer a time limited arithmetical skill testing question. Void in Quebec and wherever prohibited or restricted by law. Subject to all federal, state, local and provincial laws and regulations.

Prizes: The following values for prizes are determined by the manufacturers' suggested retail prices or by what these items are currently known to be selling for at the time this offer was published. Approximate retail values include handling and delivery of prizes. Estimated maximum retail value of prizes: 1 Grand Prize ($27,500 if merchandise or $25,000 Cash); 1 First Prize ($3,000); 5 Second Prizes ($400 each); 35 Third Prizes ($100 each); 1,000 Fourth Prizes ($9.00 each) ; 1 Early Bird Prize ($5,000); Total approximate maximum retail value is $50,000. Winners will have the option of selecting any prize offered at level won. Automobile winner must have a valid driver's license at the time the car is awarded. Trips are subject to space and departure availability. Certain black-out dates may apply. Travel must be completed within one year from the time the prize is awarded. Minors must be accompanied by an adult. Prizes won by minors will be awarded in the name of parent or legal guardian.

For a list of Major Prize Winners (available after 7/30/93): send a self-addressed, stamped envelope entirely separate from your entry to: Winners Classic Sweepstakes Winners, P.O. Box 825, Gibbstown, NJ 08027. Requests must be received by 6/1/93. DO NOT SEND ANY OTHER CORRESPONDENCE TO THIS P.O. BOX.

Women's Fiction

On Sale in January

BLUE WILLOW

29690-6 $5.50/6.50 in Canada

☐ **by Deborah Smith**

Bestselling author of MIRACLE

"Extraordinary talent.... A complex and emotionally wrenching tale that sweeps the readers on an intense rollercoaster ride through the gamut of human emotions." —*Romantic Times*

SINFUL

9312-5 $4.99/5.99 in Canada

☐ **by Susan Johnson**

Author of FORBIDDEN

"The author's style is a pleasure to read and the love scenes many and lusty!" —*Los Angeles Herald Examiner*

PRINCESS OF THE VEIL

29581-0 $4.99/5.99 in Canada

☐ **by Helen Mittermeyer**

"Intrigue, a fascinating setting, high adventure, a wonderful love story and steamy sensuality." —*Romantic Times*

LAST SUMMER

56092-1 $4.99/5.99 in Canada

☐ **by Theresa Weir**

Author of FOREVER

"An exceptional new talent...a splendid adventure that will delight readers with its realistic background and outstanding sexual tension." —*Rave Reviews*

☐ Please send me the books I have checked above I am enclosing $_____ (add $2.50 to cover postage and handling) Send check or money order, no cash or C. O. D.'s please.

Name _____

Address _____

City/ State/ Zip _____

Send order to: Bantam Books, Dept FN93, 2451 S Wolf Rd., Des Plaines, IL 60018

Allow four to six weeks for delivery Prices and availability subject to change without notice.

Ask for these books at your local bookstore or use this page to order.   FN93 2/93